'So, what's this all about, then?'

Rory folded his arms across his chest and stared at her coolly.

'What do you mean?' Sarah asked, playing for time.

'Why all the secrecy? If you're home for good, why on earth couldn't you have told us all at the reunion?'

And give him the chance to say I told you so? Not likely! Sarah lifted her chin and squared up to him in a way that he remembered well. 'Who said anything about being home for good?'

Drusilla Douglas qualified as a physiotherapist and worked happily in hospitals both north and south of the border until parental frailty obliged her to quit. When free to resume her career, she soon discovered that she had missed the boat promotion-wise. Having by then begun to dabble in romantic fiction, she worked part-time for a while at both her writing and physio, but these days considers herself more the novelist.

Recent titles by the same author:

DOCTORS IN CONFLICT

DOCTORS AT ODDS

BY
DRUSILLA DOUGLAS

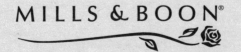

MILLS & BOON®

MILLS & BOON and MILLS & BOON with the Rose Device are registered trademarks of the publisher.

First published in Great Britain 2000
Harlequin Mills & Boon Limited,
Eton House, 18-24 Paradise Road, Richmond, Surrey TW9 1SR

© Drusilla Douglas 2000

ISBN 0 263 82246 X

Set in Times Roman 10½ on 12 pt.
03-0007-47132

Printed and bound in Spain
by Litografia Rosés, S.A., Barcelona

CHAPTER ONE

DR SARAH SINCLAIR had only popped out to get milk from the corner shop, but not far from her brother's little flat she ran straight into Dr Carrie Baxter. Neither woman could believe her eyes.

'I thought you were in Italy!' exclaimed Carrie.

'And I thought you were working in Inverness,' returned Sarah, as quick as a flash. The less said about Italy, the better.

'I still am—for the time being. The job's great, but I miss Glasgow,' revealed Carrie, blushing ever so slightly and arousing Sarah's interest. 'What brought you back here?' Carrie hurried on.

'I'm here for my brother's wedding,' said Sarah, which was true as far as it went.

Carrie seemed satisfied with that. 'I knew it couldn't be the class reunion, because Fiona told us that you were the only one she'd not been able to get hold of.'

Fiona Kerr—the born committee member of their year, and the very one to dream up a reunion five years on from graduation.

'Is everything OK with you, Sarah?' Carrie asked earnestly, having picked up the slight tension in her old friend.

'I'm very well, thank you, Doctor,' insisted Sarah with what she hoped was a convincing smile. 'Now, tell me more about the reunion.'

Carrie shrugged and said, 'They'll all be thrilled

to see you. Seven sharp tonight at the Glasgow
Metropole Hotel for drinks and dinner.'

Damn me for a fool, thought Sarah, having mis-
takenly assumed that the reunion had come and
gone. It was on the tip of her tongue to say that she
couldn't possibly make it, and then she realised that
staying away without a very good reason could look
as though she had something to hide. 'Well, if
you're quite sure it'll be all right, Carrie... It would
be really great to see everybody again,' she pretended for form's sake.

Carrie was delighted and repeated her assurances
of a great welcome for Sarah. 'Are you staying
nearby?' she asked next, and when Sarah pointed to
the flats where her brother lived, Carrie told her she
was staying just two streets away with a cousin and
would pick Sarah up at half past six.

'Thank you very much,' said Sarah, hoping she
sounded sufficiently enthusiastic. 'Better dash now,
though. Things to do...'

'And I'm on my way to get my hair done. Must
look my best. One never knows...' Again that half-
blush. 'See you later, then. I'll park by the gates and
give you three honks on the horn. Bye, now.'

Sarah frowned after Carrie and said to herself, If
only I'd been five minutes earlier. Or later. But,
then, life was a series of 'if onlys' when you thought
about it. If only she hadn't gone to Italy with Steve,
she'd not be standing here now—jobless, without
prospects and cornered into facing the questions of
her peers later on that day. For questions there
would surely be. They hadn't scrupled to tell her
she'd been mad to have gone off like that in the first
place.

*   *   *

'It's not fair,' wailed Carrie, when Sarah slid into the passenger seat beside her at the time appointed.

'What's not fair?' asked Sarah, trying not to stare at Carrie's newly gilded hairdo.

'You've not put on so much as an ounce and you look even better than you did five years ago!'

If that's true, then it's a miracle, thought Sarah. And very fortunate in view of the evening of scrutiny ahead. She tucked a stray frond of blue-black hair behind her ear and told Carrie that she was looking rather stunning herself. 'And that dress is to die for,' she added.

'So it should be, considering what it cost me,' revealed her friend. 'By the way, I phoned Fiona and she was absolutely thrilled to hear I was bringing you, so no problem. I wonder who all will turn up?'

'All our old friends, I hope,' returned Sarah robustly. She was feeling that she would cope just fine—as long as Rory Drummond wasn't there. Now that she was back in Glasgow, and seeing so many old haunts on all sides as they hurtled towards the hotel, it seemed like only yesterday that Rory had told her what a fool she was to throw away the chance of working with Professor Maxwell—'just to go dangling after that clown, who couldn't paint so much as a garden shed without botching it'. Rory had used a stronger word than 'botching'.

'Steve is the most wonderful painter!' Sarah had defended him hotly. 'And one day he's going to be famous.'

'If he is, it'll not be for anything he puts on canvas,' Rory had retorted smartly as Sarah had stormed out of his flat.

Talk of the devil—there he was now, not thirty feet away from them in the hotel car park, helping Moira Stirling out of his car. At that distance, he didn't look to have changed at all—the same lean, rangy, loose-limbed but powerful body, the same unruly brown hair, same laughing dark eyes and engaging smile. And—horror or horrors—the same ability to make Sarah's heart turn a somersault.

Carrie was taking her time about changing her driving casuals for a pair of too-tight court shoes, which left Sarah free to go on staring.

Moira, in her usual five-inch heels, was having trouble keeping her balance on the uneven cobbled ground, and she was clinging to Rory as though her life depended on him. And Rory was showing every sign of appreciating that.

'Never learn,' Carrie was saying, as she locked her car.

'Learn what? Who?' asked Sarah, who had been too busy staring to listen.

'Rory Drummond.'

So that was the way of it. 'And look! There's Kate, still chasing after Mark,' noticed Sarah. 'I'm beginning to feel as though I've never been away.'

'When *are* you going back, then?' pounced Carrie, seizing the chance, but by then they'd been spotted by some more arrivals and Sarah was able to dodge the question.

Inside the hotel Sarah contrived to mingle and laugh and then move on before the questions got too personal. It was very obvious that they'd all advanced further in their careers than she had. Those who'd stayed in hospital work were now registrars and were working for further qualifications—if they hadn't acquired them already.

Like Tom Patterson, for instance. 'I got my membership last year and Prof. Maxwell says I'm bound to get an MD for the results of my research with him,' he revealed. 'You did me a right good turn, Sarah, when you scuttled off to Italy. I'm very grateful.'

Sarah didn't care for the way he'd put that. 'I didn't exactly scuttle off, Tom. I made a—a surprising life choice, that's all.' That had sounded weak, even to herself. 'Oh, look—there's John,' she went on hurriedly. 'I thought he went to Australia. Must have a word…'

But Tom was too bulky to be squeezed round in all that crush. 'So you've no regrets, then?' he pursued relentlessly.

'We-ell,' she began unwillingly, searching for inspiration. 'Obviously, things are quite different in a foreign country…less scope for advancement if you're not a native…' She was saved by Fiona, the organiser, in her element as she leapt onto a chair so as to be heard above the din as she bade them all to find their places at table.

But only saved for a moment. Once seated, Sarah found herself next to Rory Drummond. Moira was on his other side, though, so if the grapevine had got it right he'd not be paying much attention to a back number like herself.

Almost immediately, Rory turned his back on Moira, planted an elbow on the table and supported his chin on his hand while he studied Sarah's good looks with such care that she felt herself flushing.

'Not bad—considering,' he said at last. It wasn't a good beginning.

'I wish I could be as flattering about you!' Sarah was stung into retorting.

'You've not forgiven me, then,' surmised Rory as they were served with soup.

Sarah managed a careless shrug, before asking, 'Was there something that needed forgiving? I don't remember.'

She'd done that rather well but he wasn't taken in. 'I know for sure now that I'm not forgiven,' he stated. 'Still, you've had the good sense to come home. That's something, I suppose.'

'Who says that me being here now has anything to do with going away in the first place?' Sarah asked sharply, losing some of her cool.

'Hasn't it?' Rory asked quietly, his steady brown gaze compelling her to answer.

'My brother gets married the day after tomorrow and I'm here for his wedding,' she insisted. 'Then, quite by chance this morning, I ran into Carrie and she persuaded me to come to this do. All very simple.'

'If you say so. So when are you going back?' asked Rory in the same compelling way.

'I've—not yet decided.'

'They must think very highly of you,' he said softly.

'Who?' asked Sarah, wondering what he was getting at.

'Your bosses. In Italy. If they're prepared to give you open-ended leave of absence.'

'I'm—on holiday,' Sarah improvised lamely, very grateful to the waiter who appeared at that moment

to remove their plates. 'You mustn't let me mono-
polise you,' she told Rory firmly, before turning
away to talk to the man on her other side.

Just like all the others, Angus Forbes was nicely
settled and prospering—but, then, he'd had a family
general practice to step into once he'd done the required stint in hospital. His eyes brightened with a
sudden thought. 'We'll soon be looking for another
partner, if you're interested, Sarah. As I remember,
you always had a bent for general medicine.'

Must be why I got the gold medal for it, Sarah
thought wryly as she started on the coq au vin. And
much good it did me... 'Thanks, Angus. I might
well be interested,' she told him quietly, in case
Rory should overhear. Not that that was very likely
now that he was chatting so brightly with Moira.

'Super,' said Angus, passing Sarah his menu.
'Write your address and telephone number on this.
We must keep in touch.'

'He's married now, you know,' Rory whispered
in Sarah's ear as the main course plates were removed.

'Who is?' she asked, turning surprised midnight
blue eyes his way.

'Angus, of course. And she's a very nice girl so
don't you go getting any ideas.'

Sarah was furious, but she bit back the retort hov-
ering on her lips. She mustn't let him see how easily
he could still rile her. 'Really, Rory, how absurd can
you get?' she asked lightly. 'We were only agreeing
to keep in touch. Where's the harm in that? We were
good friends once.'

He shrugged. 'Just thought I'd warn you in case
you made a fool of yourself—that's all.'

He'd really got to her now. 'This is the second time you've had the nerve to warn me not to make a fool of myself,' she flared. 'There'd better not be a third. Who the hell do you think you are?' Sarah knew she was over-reacting, but he'd always had more power than most to needle her.

'During the soup, you were claiming not to remember the first time,' he reminded her slyly.

'You are absolutely impossible!' hissed Sarah.

'Is that a fact?' he said, lifting an eyebrow in that irritating way he had. 'And here I was thinking it was the other way about. I don't know what's been happening to you these past few years, but one thing's certain. It's not done much for your temper.'

How could she have forgotten how skilful he was at turning the tables? 'Damn you, Rory Drummond!' she fumed to his broad back when he turned away as Moira reclaimed his attention.

'Don't fret, Sarah—Rory means well,' said Angus comfortingly, who had tuned in for that last exchange. 'Fact is, he always had a soft spot for you, you know. Like most of us boys.'

'Thanks, Angus, you're a dear. All the same, there's no getting away from the fact that Rory Drummond is about as irritating as they come,' declared Sarah, as a rather tired-looking individual raspberry pavlova was set before her. Why was it that the food at dinners like these was often so unexciting?

Over coffee afterwards, Sarah was able to talk to many more old friends. None of them was half as unsettling as Rory Drummond had been, and they all accepted her cover story about being home for a family wedding.

It was getting late and the crowd was beginning to thin out when a rather apologetic Carrie came looking for Sarah. 'Look, love,' she began awkwardly, 'I feel awful, having brought you, but would you mind getting a taxi home? The thing is, I've been getting on rather well with Robin Tait. Remember Robin? And he's offered me a lift...'

Sarah hid a tiny smile as she remembered how Carrie had always hankered after Robin. 'No problem,' she insisted. 'I wouldn't dream of queering your pitch. You have fun now.'

Carrie gave Sarah a quick hug, told her what a darling she was and skipped happily off. Too late, Sarah thought, to ask why she didn't drive herself home in Carrie's car and park it outside the cousin's house. It would have saved them both a lot of trouble. I've lost all my initiative, while pandering to a neurotic painter, she supposed. Well, I'd damn well better find it again before I go job-hunting!

She found a phone booth in the hotel foyer and ordered a taxi. A cheerful voice promised it would be there in less than ten minutes, so she turned up the collar of her thin foreign jacket and emerged into the cool of a summer night in Glasgow. The taxi took longer than that, though, and Sarah was still shivering on the hotel steps when an elderly metallic grey Audi shot past, screeched to a halt and then reversed. Rory Drummond stepped out and called across, 'Having trouble, Sarah?'

'No, not really,' she claimed. 'Just waiting for my lift.'

'You'll be lucky. Carrie went off with Robin Tait some time ago.'

Was there nothing he missed? 'I know that. I've ordered a taxi.'

'That was ages ago.' How did he know *that*? 'So it's obviously not coming. Meanwhile, you must be freezing to death in that thin thing you're wearing. You'd better come with us.'

Sarah fully intended to refuse until she saw how much Moira was fuming in the front seat. They had never got on, so for no other reason than to annoy her some more Sarah said, 'Well, thanks, Rory—if you're sure it's no bother.' Then she skipped across the wide pavement to the car.

'Where to—Regent Terrace?' he asked as they set off.

Sarah was ridiculously pleased that he remembered where she used to live. There had been a time when he'd been a frequent visitor… She pulled herself together and told him, 'Further than that, I'm afraid. I'm staying with Bruce at his flat in Maitland Crescent.'

'You're going the wrong way for Maitland Crescent,' said Moira shrilly when Rory turned right at the end of the road.

'It's all right, I know what I'm doing,' he returned easily. 'Where's the point in dragging you halfway across the city and back at this time of night when you live three streets away from here?'

'Are you saying you're going to drop me off *first*?'

'Got it in one,' he confirmed.

'Well, I'm not having it!' stormed Moira. 'I'm the one you brought to that boring do, so—'

'Oh, come on, girl, you know it makes sense,' he teased, making Moira crosser than ever. 'Especially when you've been telling me for the past half-hour how tired you are after a hard day at work at that private hospital of yours.'

Trust Moira to find herself a cushy little number, thought Sarah as Moira raved, 'That was only because... Oh, hell! Have it your own way. You usually do!'

What had she almost said? Sarah wondered avidly. Only because she wanted to get him away from the others and all to herself? That would account for her fury when he picked her up. Yet the way Carrie told it, the keenness is all on the other side...

Moira maintained a sulky silence until Rory drew up outside her house. He got out to see her to her door, where it took him the best part of three minutes to say goodnight.

'I'm sorry if I've kept you waiting,' he said politely when he returned.

'Oh, no, not at all,' responded Sarah with equal courtesy. 'I'm only too grateful for the lift.'

'Then how about showing your gratitude by getting into the front?' he suggested, sounding more like himself. 'Back-seat passengers always make me feel like I'm in the taxi business.'

Sarah did as he'd asked and they set off again. 'The evening went very well, I thought,' she offered after a few minutes of a silence that was becoming awkward.

'As well as could be expected, I'd say,' offered Rory in exchange. 'It was certainly a good turn-out.'

'And everybody doing so well—at least, all those I managed to get a word with.' What on earth had prompted her to go down that road? Now he'd be sure to ask how *she* was doing! 'Thank heaven you

noticed me shivering outside the hotel afterwards,'
she dashed on feverishly. 'And I'm very sorry if
Moira minded.'

'Why would she?' he asked. 'This is my car and
I can invite whom I please into it.'

Having diverted him, as she thought, Sarah relaxed and asked, 'So what are you doing these days,
Rory?'

'For the present I'm on Professor Carlisle's team
at the City Hospital. And he's being really decent to
me.'

Sarah wasn't surprised to hear that. Whatever else
he might be, Rory Drummond was clever, consci-
entious and very hard-working. 'And, of course,
you've got your fellowship,' she assumed. 'That
goes without saying. Do you mean to stick with orthopaedics, then?'

'I certainly do, though eventually perhaps with a
bias towards trauma rather than elective surgery.' He
chuckled quietly. 'I always did like mending things.
Now it's your turn to tell me what you're up to these
days, Sarah.'

She should have remembered how difficult it was
to divert him. 'Oh, general medicine—same as always,' she answered vaguely.

'And is the set-up in Naples similar to ours?'

Why did she have the feeling that he was setting
a trap for her? 'Sure. Well, more or less...' She had
no intention of admitting that she'd spent less than
a year in that wonderful, shining new hospital before
Steve had dragged her all round the poorer but very
picturesque south of Italy in search of inspiration for
his paintings, which had just got more and more

weird… Sarah's last job had been in a charity clinic, run on a shoestring by nuns.

'You're not giving much away, are you?' asked Rory perceptively. 'Are you afraid I'll suspect that it's not been all roses out there?'

'It's a bit too hot for roses where I've been working,' Sarah retorted, while she wondered how to get out of this awkward conversation. 'Don't you worry about me, Rory Drummond,' she said. 'I'm doing just fine.'

'But not in Naples,' he said, quietly but firmly.

'Who says?' Sarah asked crisply.

'Fiona. When she wrote to the Ospitale di Napoli to invite you to the reunion, the letter came back marked with the Italian equivalent of "not known".'

'I…see,' said Sarah in a stifled voice.

'I think that perhaps I do, too,' returned Rory as he stopped the car where Sarah had indicated. Then, having turned and laid a restraining hand on her arm, he said seriously, 'Listen, please, Sarah. I'm not going to preach—you told me off too damn well the last time I tried. I just want you to remember that when you went away you left behind some very good friends here in Glasgow. Real friends, who'd be very glad to—to have you back.'

Sarah was assailed by all sorts of emotions—gratitude and nostalgia were two of them—but the strongest of all was the desire to keep her pride intact. 'I'm sure you meant that kindly, Rory,' she said tautly after a minute's thought, 'but, despite what you think you know, I'm not in any trouble. Neither do I have any plans to come back to Glasgow.' Then she got out of the car before he could unsettle her some more. 'Thank you very much for the lift. See you at the next reunion perhaps?'

'Who knows?' he asked neutrally. 'Nice seeing you at this one, anyway. Take care—and good luck.'

He'd set the car in motion before he'd finished speaking.

CHAPTER TWO

SARAH hoisted her empty cases up on top of the wardrobe, before looking round the little room. It wasn't exactly cosy, but after several weeks of job-hunting a resident SHO locum on Dr Marshall's general medical wards at Allanbank Hospital on Glasgow's east side was not to be sneezed at. Her aim had been to start her new life well away from her home town, but time was pressing. Her slender savings were almost exhausted and she'd been feeling like the proverbial gooseberry since her brother and his wife had returned from their honeymoon.

The deciding factor had been finding out that nobody from her year was working here, so if she got the job she'd applied for in England she'd soon be away again and the old crowd could go on believing that she'd gone back to Italy and Steve.

Steve. The biggest mistake of her life so far and one that had cost her so much in so many ways...

The shrilling of the phone on the bedside table pulled Sarah back to the present. 'Dr Sinclair? Sister Gordon, ward twelve here. I know you're not down to start until tomorrow, but a patient admitted with asthma and bronchitis seems to be having a CVA, so—'

'On my way,' promised Sarah, grabbing her white coat and discovering how good it felt to be on her way to her first case back home in Scotland.

The diagnosis was obvious before she'd tested re-

19

flexes, muscle tone, visual reactions or conscious-
ness level—a drooping cheek and stertorous
breathing were enough. 'Yes, Sister, a typical left-
sided hemiparesis,' confirmed Sarah. 'Does she have
any history of CVA?'

'Not to my knowledge, Doctor. Mrs Begg is one
of our regulars as regards her chest condition, but
there's nothing much else in her notes.'

'Right. We'll set up the usual routine observation
and you can let me know if there's any change in
her vital signs or BP. I'll be on the unit for the next
couple of hours, going over things with the registrar.' It then occurred to Sarah to ask why she and
not the registrar had been called to this patient.

'I'm afraid Dr Gray's not in today, Doctor. She's
having a difficult pregnancy.'

What have I walked into here? wondered Sarah,
before saying humorously, 'And as I'm standing in
for your SHO, who's been in a car crash, I'd better
be careful—things are said to go in threes. I hope
the consultant is quite well?'

Sister laughed heartily and said that a doctor with
a sense of humour was just what the unit needed,
and that Dr Marshall was taking a clinic if Sarah
wanted to give him the once-over.

Sarah drew the line at that but decided to go and
report this emergency, together with a résumé of her
treatment. SHOs weren't expected to exercise too
much initiative.

Dr Marshall was very pleased with that display of
forethought. 'It's a pity about Dr Gray,' he said next,
'but I've arranged for the unit nursing officer to
show you around instead.'

One brief look told Sarah that Miss Coull was one

of the old school and probably not far off retirement. She straight away apologised for keeping the UNO waiting. 'I was called to a patient who was having a CVA—a fairly serious one,' she emphasised, 'so I hope you'll forgive me for being late. And as I'm the only doctor on duty, I'm afraid I'll have to break off every so often to check on her.'

'You appear to have settled in remarkably quickly for someone who wasn't expected until tomorrow, Doctor,' said Miss Coull, as though she found that cause for disapproval.

'Hobson's choice,' Sarah returned matter-of-factly, 'with the registrar off sick and the newly qualified house officer sitting in with the consultant.'

Dr Marshall's unit was not large—just seventy beds in two wards—but Miss Coull insisted on showing Sarah everything down to the smallest cupboard. 'No empty beds, I see,' Sarah remarked when the tour was over, 'and summertime too. What happens in winter if there's a serious flu epidemic?'

Miss Coull said they would just have to wait and see, but why was Sarah bothered? She'd be away from the hospital long before then!

And thank heaven for that, thought Sarah, watching the retreating figure. You certainly know how to put folk in their place!

Two weeks on, the end of June, and Sarah had never worked so hard in her life. The registrar was absent at least half the time and the junior houseman was only allowed to do the most basic routine tasks. The previous night, Sarah had been duty SHO for all the medical wards, which had meant hardly any sleep. After a quick shower, a change of clothes and a

hurried breakfast, she arrived on her own unit, sti-
fling a yawn.

'A heavy night,' guessed Jack Kinnear, the
friendly charge nurse on the men's ward.

'And how!' agreed Sarah with another yawn. 'So
I'll be much obliged if you'll arrange for a nice easy
day.'

'You'll be lucky.' He smiled. 'I was just about to
buzz you when you appeared. Old Charlie Greig fell
in the loo a few minutes ago, and now he's in a lot
of pain with his left hip.' He frowned. 'He's had
quite a lot of steroids over the years so—'

'Say no more—just lead the way,' said Sarah with
a sigh.

It was pretty obvious that the fall that resulted in
a fractured neck of femur, despite the old man's
plucky insistence that 'it's nobbut a wee bit bruising,
hen'.

'Let's hope you're right, Mr Greig,' said Sarah,
'but just to be on the safe side, huh?'

Moving away from the bedside, she said in a low
voice to Jack, 'I'll give him something for the pain
and then we'd better get him X-rayed and call in the
orthopods. They may want to fix him up today.'

'I doubt that,' said Jack. 'Today's the day the registrars change over, so they'll be a bit pushed.'

'Change over?' echoed Sarah. 'I don't understand.'

'A year here, a year there—Professor Carlisle
likes to keep them on the move.'

'I see.' She shrugged. 'Well, pushed or not,
they'll need to deal with Charlie p.d.q. Their SHO,
Dr Blair, is a nice bloke, so I'll give him a ring.

He's better placed than we are to speed things up.'
She went at once to the phone.

It wasn't long before a radiographer arrived, trundling the not so lightweight portable machine. She
was actually X-raying Charlie's hip when the orthopaedic team arrived to see him.

When Sarah caught sight of the new registrar, she
all but dived under the nearest bed. What had she
done to deserve such devilish luck?

She couldn't get out of the ward because the orthopods were between her and the door so, cursing
the need for such a loss of dignity, she bolted into
the cleaners' utility room, where she hovered with
the door on the crack so that she could hear what
was said.

'Where's your registrar?' That was Rory
Drummond's first question for Jack as they stood
there, waiting for the radiographer to finish.

'Off sick,' explained Jack, 'but the SHO was here
a moment ago. Called away, I expect. Shall I bleep
her?'

'Not for the moment,' decided Rory, to Sarah's
intense relief. That had been a near thing. How
would she have explained if he'd said yes and she'd
been flushed out of such a hiding place?

The sound of more trundling suggested that the
X-ray session was over and then Rory was asking
the radiographer to get the plates processed as soon
as possible as he needed to be sure of the diagnosis,
before booking a theatre. 'We'll come and look at
them in your department in about half an hour,' he
went on. 'Or do I ask too much?'

'Absolutely not,' gushed the girl, bringing a wry
smile to Sarah's face. So Rory Drummond was still

having the effect she remembered on the young and impressionable.

Next, as always when speaking to patients, his tone was kind and reassuring. 'I'm afraid you've given this hip of yours a nasty bang,' he began, 'and if, as I suspect, you've broken a bone, we'll need to fix it under anaesthetic. I hope that's all right with you?'

'Anything you say, Doctor,' Charlie agreed, 'so long as you make a good job of it, mind.'

Some surgeons would have gone through the roof at that, but Rory was amused. 'I've not had any complaints so far.' He chuckled. 'And as I'm not aiming to spoil my record, I'd say you're fairly safe. It'll probably be the afternoon or early evening before we can get a theatre, though—I hope that's OK with you.'

'Aye, I reckon,' said Charlie without any proviso this time.

The voices grew fainter as the team left the ward, so it was safe for Sarah to come out of hiding. There was plenty of work waiting to be done—another new admission to be examined and charted and different antibiotics to be prescribed for patients who weren't responding to the original choice.

One of them had also developed a productive cough, so Sarah wrote him up for some physiotherapy. And, heaven help her, the houseman hadn't finished taking routine blood samples yet! She helped him with those and still managed to squeeze in a check on the patient who'd had a stroke on Sarah's first day. Everything had to be ready for the consultant's round that afternoon.

When speeding to the canteen for lunch, Sarah

stopped dead on a sudden thought. Rory might be
there and she'd rather not run into him until she'd
thought up a good reason for being here. So she
went instead to buy sandwiches from the snack bar
in Outpatients. Returning to the unit and opening the
door of the doctors' room, she found Rory lounging
at the desk and resting his feet on the wastepaper
bin. She stood there in the doorway, speechless with
annoyance and embarrassment, while he—the
wretch—was as calm and unruffled as ever.

'I was told I'd find you somewhere about up
here,' he said mildly.

'But…how?' croaked Sarah, when she'd mastered
the constriction in her throat.

'How did I know you were here? Would you believe from your signature on Charlie Greig's X-ray
request form? There couldn't be two Sarah J.
Sinclairs with identical handwriting.' He got to his
feet, folded his arms across his chest and stared at
her coolly. 'So, what's this all about, then?'

'What do you mean?' she asked, playing for time.

'Why all the secrecy? If you're home for good,
why on earth couldn't you have told us all at the
reunion?'

And give him the chance to say I told you so?
Not likely! Sarah lifted her chin and squared up to
him in a way that he remembered well. 'Who said
anything about being home for good?' she asked
haughtily. 'The thing is…I'm taking a break between jobs, if you must know. To see the family.
After all, it's nearly four years since I—went away.'

'And your idea of a break between Italian jobs is
a locum in Glasgow, is it?' asked Rory, blowing a
hole in her cover story straight away. 'And it can't

be easy keeping up with the family either now that your mother has moved down to Surrey, near your sister,' he added, demolishing her tale completely.

'How did you know that?' Sarah demanded angrily.

He ignored her question to ask again, 'Why the secrecy?'

Sarah felt herself flushing and hated him for it. When she'd managed at last to drag her eyes away from his accusing brown ones, she said, 'All right, then—I did let everybody assume that I was going back to Italy, but I changed my mind, that's all. People are allowed to, you know. Change their minds, that is.'

'Absolutely,' he agreed. 'So why all the secrecy?' he asked a third time.

'I'm not being secretive,' Sarah claimed.

'Oh, yes, you are,' he insisted. 'And, believe me, that's the best possible way to set folk wondering what you're trying to hide. If things out there went badly wrong, as I suspect is the case—'

He was quite right about that, but he could whistle for the details! 'Thank you very much for your advice,' she interrupted sarcastically. 'I shall do my best to profit by it. And now, if you don't mind, I should like to have my lunch.'

'Just what I was going to suggest,' Rory said easily. 'I'm told the canteen here is better than most. Ready?'

'You've heard aright about the canteen,' she confirmed, 'and as it's Thursday I'd recommend the haggis, but I'm having sandwiches here while I catch up on the paperwork.'

Rory eyed her steadily for what felt like half an

hour, before saying, 'I wasn't going to quiz you, Sarah, though that's obviously what you were expecting. Still, even without knowing all the details, I'm pretty sure you've done the right thing in making the break.' He left leaving her all churned up with rage and humiliation.

Charlie Greig had his fractured neck of femur pinned and plated that evening, and when Sarah checked him over afterwards he was full of praise for 'that grand young chap' who'd fixed him up. 'He'll go far, I reckon,' said Charlie.

And the sooner the better, thought Sarah, although the damage had been done now. Naturally, Rory would tell his girlfriend that Sarah had left Steve and was working at the Allanbank. Moira would then rush to tell everybody she could get hold of and any minute now the phone calls would begin.

When Monday came without any such calls, Sarah realised that Rory must be keeping her secret. She was grateful for that, but went on smarting because he had been the one to find her out. Discovery would have been more bearable from anybody else.

Out of thoughts like that came the question, Am I making too much of this? After all, what was she hiding? Only that she'd finally left a man who'd never been more to her than second best—a man she would have left before but for her reluctance to admit that she'd made a mistake.

The one person from whom she'd most wanted to hide her failure had found her out because, even without knowing the details, he'd arrived at the right conclusion. So leaving Glasgow was no longer the imperative it had seemed. Rory had been right when he'd reminded her how many good friends she had here—and now that *he* knew, it wouldn't be too difficult to confess to the others.

That was definitely something to consider, but not now. Tonight she was on call again, so she'd better go and get something to eat while things were relatively quiet.

Hardly anybody lived in nowadays and the canteen was almost empty. Unfortunately, Rory was there with his SHO, Peter Blair, but they were deep in discussion and, given luck, they wouldn't notice her. Quietly, Sarah collected a cheese salad and a coffee, and headed for a table out of Rory's line of vision. He spotted her, though, and called her over.

With nothing to be done but comply, Sarah made the best of it. 'You're working late are you not, m'lad?' she asked, taking the initiative.

'Are you suggesting I'm a nine-to-five man? Dinnae you be sae cheeky, lassie!' he returned with pretended outrage. 'And if it's all the same to you, Pete and I have only just finished the round of today's theatre cases.'

'Do you two know each other?' asked the SHO curiously.

'Very well indeed as it happens. We trained together,' explained Rory.

Peter was amazed. 'But you're a registrar and Sarah's only…' He stumbled to a stop, embarrassed by his tactlessness.

'That's because Sarah threw up a potentially brilliant career to go and work abroad,' said Rory, before Sarah could come up with something convincing.

Peter took that to mean a mercy mission to the

Third World. 'Good Lord, how marvellous,' he enthused. 'I used to think I'd like to do something like
that, but with competition so fierce for the best
jobs—'

'And you being a married man with twins, it
wouldn't have made sense,' Rory finished for him.
'Mind you, I'd not be surprised to hear that Sarah
is regretting her quixotic impulse—and that's why
she's come home to try and kick-start her career
again.'

'S-something like that,' she agreed faintly, unsure
whether she was most surprised or most grateful for
Rory's skilful intervention. He'd certainly saved her
from any more awkward questions at this hospital.

'Well, I'd better push off or there'll be nothing
left of the evening,' Rory was saying now. 'Don't
forget what I said about that meniscectomy, will
you, Pete? Nice meeting you again, Sarah. We must
make time for a chat and get up to date.'

'Great guy,' said Peter, as they watched Rory
cover the distance to the door in long easy strides
and then shoulder his way through the swing doors
in that special way he had. 'I'm really glad he's
here. He knows such a lot and doesn't mind sharing
his knowledge—unlike some!' His bleeper began a
mournful cheeping and he sighed. 'That makes
twice since I sat down. It's a wonder all junior doctors don't end up with gastric problems. See you
around, Sarah.'

'Yes—I hope so,' she responded mechanically.
Her mind was still busy with the skilful way that
Rory had explained her relatively junior position
here. That had been really kind. But, then, to be fair,
hadn't he always been ready to do a kindness? It

had been something that had deceived her young, green, untried self into thinking he'd felt something special for her. He hadn't, though, although they'd become friends. Until she'd taken up with Steve.

Why had she? At least she knew the answer to that. It was *because* Rory hadn't found her special, while Steve had showered her with thoughtful and touching attention. She'd encouraged him in the hope of making Rory jealous, but all she'd done had been to incite his contempt.

'If you can't have the man you love, then take the man who loves you,' a rather simplistic granny had once told her. So that was what Sarah had done, only to find out that Steve hadn't been quite as devoted as she'd thought—once he'd made his conquest. For a long time, before making the break, she'd been little more to him than a meal ticket, leaving him free to indulge his passion for painting.

The canteen was now almost empty and Sarah's forgotten coffee was cold. She put her used dishes on the trolley provided and went to the residents' sitting room to await the next call. It wasn't long in coming.

Thursday was Dr Marshall's ward round day, and today he was in what the staff called his picky mood and everybody was coming in for it.

It was the physio's turn now. 'How long have you been treating this man, Mrs Clarke?'

'One week and four days, Dr Marshall,' she returned, knowing that to say almost a fortnight would never have done on a day like this.

'And he still needs a Zimmer?'

'His balance isn't good enough for sticks, or even elbow crutches.'

'So what are you doing about his balance?'

'The usual free and resisted exercises—both with and without the aid of a mirror—but I gather from Dr Sinclair that there's some question of a cerebellar lesion so I'm not looking for much improvement. Just aiming to keep him safe.'

'Yet I'm told that he fell again the day before yesterday.'

'That was one of the times he got excited and forgot his instructions.'

'Then write them down for him.'

'I do—every day—in case he mislays them. I've also made a tape for his Walkman.'

Unable to think of any more pinpricks for Polly Clarke, the consultant turned his attention to Sarah. 'I don't suppose you've managed to get a neurologist to see him yet, Doctor?'

'He came just before the round, sir, and agrees with our findings, so Mr Montgomerie is booked for a scan the day after tomorrow. Unfortunately, the daughter with whom he lives also has a disabled husband, and she doesn't think she can go on looking after both of them so she's asked if there's any chance of long-term care.'

'For both of them?'

'No, Dr Marshall. For her father.'

'Always make your meaning clear, Doctor. Clarity is vital in medicine,' Sarah was informed. 'You may tell the daughter that we'll cross that bridge when we come to it. Her father isn't nearly ready for discharge yet. Next, please!'

'He should have been a bank teller,' Polly Clarke

whispered to Sarah as they made their way to the women's ward.

Dr Marshall was unable to fault anybody over Mrs Begg's treatment, she who had been Sarah's first patient at the Allanbank. Mrs Begg was now able to walk the length of the ward with the aid of a quadropod, a four-pronged walking stick.

'But can she wash and dress herself, Mrs Clarke?' asked the great man after this display of mobility.

'If she takes her time,' she answered.

'Except for fiddly wee buttons,' corrected the patient.

'Keep her until the weekend and then let her go home,' decided Dr Marshall, 'but see her twice a week to make sure she doesn't regress.'

He led his retinue to the next patient. 'I don't suppose you've done that lumbar puncture I asked for yet, Dr Sinclair?'

'Right after Dr Gray rang to tell me she'd not be in today,' Sarah answered, thus reminding him that, firstly, they were understaffed and, secondly, that senior house officers weren't usually expected to do lumbar punctures.

'Attagirl,' breathed Polly admiringly, as Dr Marshall harrumphed on both counts.

He kept up the attack, though, and to show her displeasure Sister Gordon declined to offer coffee when the round was over.

'I suppose you think I was rather hard on the staff today,' said the consultant, following Sarah to the doctors' room. 'But even the best of them can occasionally get complacent, so it does no harm to ginger them up now and again—as you'll discover if you're ever a consultant.'

'Quite, sir,' Sarah agreed, although she'd rather he'd said 'when', not 'if'.

'Sir, about Mrs Aitken,' she added hurriedly when he looked like dashing off.

'Remind me,' he ordered.

'The lady in bay four with long-standing bronchiectasis, who also has that terrible arthritic knee. You decided to refer her to Mr Murray with a view to joint replacement, and as Mr Murray likes to get his referrals at consultant level...' Sarah held out the appropriate form for his signature.

'Thank you for reminding me, Sarah—especially as I'll be going to that conference next week.'

'I know, but what if Dr Gray isn't back?' she asked firmly.

'Alternative cover will be arranged,' he told her loftily. 'Although, from what I've seen of your work so far, you are quite capable of acting up.'

Sarah would have liked to have said that compliments were all very well, but not enough when you were doing two jobs most of the time. However, she merely said, 'Thank you, sir, I'm very flattered.' She'd be needing a good reference when her time was up here.

Charlie Greig managed to slide off the commode during the night, despite the best efforts of the nurse in attendance. 'He just sort of slipped through my hands,' she wailed. 'I couldn't stop him going, but I did manage to stop him going down with a bump.'

'Considering he's twice your size, you did very well, then,' comforted Sarah. 'All the same, we'd better get him X-rayed to be on the safe side.' Charlie was almost certainly none the worse for his

tumble, but Sarah was taking no chances with someone so accident-prone. She asked for the X-ray report to be sent straight to Orthopaedics for scrutiny
and then, with Charlie off her mind, she got on with
a day that proved to be as hectic as any other.

'Six with diarrhoea so far this morning,' reported
Sister Gordon. 'They're all blaming yesterday's
lunch, but as it's only bay two that's affected I'm
wondering if it was something brought in from outside. I found this bit of pork pie in Mrs Allan's
locker and it looks distinctly iffy to me.'

'It smells iffy as well,' said Sarah, having taken
a sniff. 'You'd better send it to the lab with any
samples of stool. Meanwhile, I'd better take a look
at the sufferers to exclude anything more sinister.'

All seemed to be straightforward, but the exami-
nations took time Sarah didn't have to spare and she
was late starting her ward round. This in turn made
her late in Outpatients, and only by cutting lunch
did she manage to write up two new admissions before the consultant got to work on them.

'Any ideas, Sarah?' he asked afterwards.

She knew she was sticking her neck out and could
be shot down, but she answered candidly, 'Both patients are elderly and both have been taking such a
cocktail of pills for this and that—mostly bought
over the counter—that I'm bound to wonder if at
least some of their troubles are due to side effects.'

'You could well be right,' he said, to her relief.
'Multiple dosing is one of the main problems of
modern medicine, so we'll withdraw all medication,
observe closely and treat any significant symptoms
as they occur. Is that clear?'

'Yes, thank you, sir.' At the risk of annoying him,

Sarah felt obliged to repeat her worries about cover during his absence. 'Please, what should I do if Dr Gray *isn't* here next week, Dr Marshall? After all, I'm only the SHO...'

'You're so able that I'm inclined to forget that,' he said cheerfully. 'I'll have a word with Dr Cairns, the most senior of the medical registrars, just in case. Oh, and before I forget, look in on Fergus Grant, an old patient of mine in surgical six, will you? They've done all they can for him and now they'd like us to take him over. The usual story—they're crying out for beds.' He was away like the wind before Sarah could remind him that their wards were also full.

Still, orders were orders—even impossible ones— so Sarah paid the required visit to ward six, sympathised with their bed shortage, outlined her own similar problem and promised to let them know the minute she had a free bed.

As she was whizzing through Outpatients on her way back to base, Rory came out of a consulting room. He fell into step beside her, obliging her to slow down. 'You're a bit off the beaten track, are you not?' he asked with a smile.

'Just taking the quickest way back from Surgical.'

'I didn't think you'd come looking for me,' he returned, picking up the vibes. 'Still, as I'm on my way to see old Charlie, I may as well walk with you. If you don't object?'

'Why would I object?' asked Sarah.

'For no reason I can think of, but one never knows—with you.'

'You're making me sound like an unexploded bomb,' she protested.

'That's rather a good analogy,' Rory returned so promptly that Sarah wished she'd never thought of it.

'Was there something significant on Charlie's X-ray, then?' she asked, moving to safer ground.

'No, he'd got away with it this time, but I'd been thinking of calling on the old chap and, seeing that film on my desk, it reminded me.'

'He'll be very pleased,' said Sarah. 'He thinks you're the bee's knees.'

He grinned crookedly. 'Oddly enough, I do have that effect on *some* people.'

'Tell me something new,' she suggested.

Rory took her at her word. 'OK, how about this? Carrie Baxter and Robin Tait were seen dining together twice last week.'

Seen by whom? wondered Sarah. By Rory himself and Moira Stirling, no doubt. 'I thought Carrie was working in Inverness,' she said.

'So what? She obviously thinks that Robin is worth the trip up and down the A9 on her evenings off. He must be very flattered. A man likes to think he's worth a bit of trouble.'

'What men think and what men *are*—those are two different things,' Sarah said firmly.

'That's very cynical, Sarah,' Rory told her censoriously.

'Possibly. It's true, though.'

'It sounds to me as though you could do with a Robin Tait in your life,' he told her, glancing sideways to gauge the effect of his words.

She very nearly told him to mind his own damned business, but she bit back the words and managed lightly, 'Too bad that Carrie got in first, then. Robin's off limits now.'

'You'd never poach—or otherwise go out of your way to get a man, would you, Sarah?' asked Rory, sounding quite serious for a change.

'Absolutely not!' she declared. 'Then he couldn't accuse me of throwing myself at him when things went wrong!'

After a moment he said, 'Just because things went wrong for you once, there's no reason to suppose they always will.'

'Trust you to put the least favourable construction on my innocent remark! But here's another point. There's enough misery going around, without me adding to it by pinching somebody's else's man.'

'Very true and very noble but supposing... supposing a mutual attraction should flare up while you—or the man—were already seeing somebody else?'

'Then he'd damn well need to deal with his somebody else before taking up with me. As I said, I'm no poacher.'

'I think I was the one who said that,' Rory reminded her, 'but never mind. I take your point.'

'What's up now?' he asked, when she stopped dead where the corridor divided, trying to ignore the strong attraction she felt for him.

'I go this way—a patient to see in the women's ward. See you, Rory.'

'I expect so,' he said with a shrug.

CHAPTER THREE

SHE didn't, though. A whole week went by without Sarah and Rory coming face to face. She caught glimpses of him—across the canteen, way off down a corridor or out of a window—but they were never near enough for them to speak. Sarah was disappointed and she put that down to the fact that she knew very few of the staff and he was at least a familiar face.

When he heard that Sarah would be off the coming weekend, her brother insisted that she should use his flat as he and his wife would be visiting her family. Sarah was glad to accept. She couldn't think what she would find to do, but it would be lovely to sleep in a comfortable bed without a telephone two feet from her ear.

On Saturday morning, just as she had more than six weeks previously, Sarah ran into Carrie Baxter while on her way to the corner shop. Carrie was looking very excited and happy.

'You look as though you've won the lottery,' said Sarah, before Carrie could ask her why she was still in Glasgow.

'Much better than that,' trilled Carrie. 'Robin and I are getting married.'

Sarah hugged her friend and cried, 'Oh, Carrie! I'm so happy for you. When's it to be?'

'We haven't got round to that yet, but I've left Inverness and moved in with him while we think.

What about you, though? We all thought you'd be back in Italy long before this.'

The moment of truth! 'Yes, well… Listen, Carrie, you're not to laugh at me or anything, but I'm doing an SHO medical job at the Allanbank. While I have a—a think,' she added lamely.

When she'd taken that in, Carrie asked, 'Why the blazes would I laugh at you, Sarah? If you want my opinion, that's the most sensible thing you've done since—well, for ages!'

'You're not the first person to tell me that,' said Sarah, thinking of Rory. 'But what are you doing in these parts? Visiting your cousin?'

Carrie looked puzzled until the penny dropped. 'No! Robin lives in the flats opposite your brother's place.'

'I never knew that.'

'Well, you wouldn't, hen. He only moved in the week after the reunion. Listen, why don't we catch up over a coffee in that wee café? I'd ask you back, only Robin's studying this morning.'

'I've got a better idea,' said Sarah. 'I've got Bruce's place to myself this weekend, so why not come back with me?'

Fortunately Carrie, who was usually so curious, was too full of her own happy situation to want to dig deeply, and she accepted without question Sarah's brief account of disillusionment with Steve and dissatisfaction with her dead-end job in Italy. 'So now I just want to put it all behind me and get on with my life,' she ended, thinking, Just listen to yourself, Sarah Sinclair! With lines like that, you could write a soap opera, if you fail at medicine!

'I should jolly well think you do—and it sounds

as though you've made a good start,' approved
Carrie, taking it all at face value. 'But you need a
social life, too, so you'd better come round to our
place tonight—just a few friends for a celebratory
drink and some supper.'

Sarah was immensely grateful, both for Carrie's
forbearance and her invitation. 'Thank you, Carrie,
dear, I'd love to come. As you said yourself, I could
do with a bit of social life.'

They talked for a while longer—mostly about
Robin and how wonderful he was—then Carrie said
she must go and make him some lunch.

Sarah hadn't bargained for a party and she'd left
her only decent dress at the hospital, so she caught
a bus to Buchanan Street and came back with a simple and inexpensive sheath of some ruby red silky
stuff, which looked rather spectacular with her long,
shining black hair and a Mediterranean tan which
had faded now to palest gold.

Robin's brother, James, certainly thought so and
he monopolised Sarah the moment they were introduced. James was on leave from the Navy and he
kept Sarah entertained with tales of his travels. They
were comparing notes on Naples when Rory arrived—alone. He stood in the doorway, looking
round the room. Meeting Sarah's gaze, he nodded
briefly, before edging round the crush to speak to
two girls who'd been waving and shouting out to
him. Sarah didn't recognise either of them.

'Good old Rory, keeping up the good work,' declared James, following Rory's progress. 'The cute
little blonde one is a nurse at the City Hospital and
her father is Rory's boss. Robin's, too, of course.
There are plenty of hopefuls in the running for that

little darling, but Rory is said to be flavour of the month.'

'You know an awful lot for a sailor who only gets home twice a year,' Sarah remarked somewhat tartly.

'I'm also a medic—didn't I say? But, then, I thought you'd know that.'

'I knew that Robin had two brothers and that one was also a doctor—I just assumed that you were the other one.'

'God forbid! Archie followed the old man into the Church! I suppose you wouldn't like to go and find a disco or something?'

'Great fun, I'm sure, but would it not look rather rude?' asked Sarah. 'This is supposed to be their engagement party and nobody's proposed a toast yet.'

James looked guilty. 'Good Lord, I was supposed to do that—thanks for the reminder.'

He did it very wittily, getting a lot of laughs for himself and some very warm, if ribald good wishes for Carrie and Robin. Then Fiona called out for the table to be cleared so that she could bring in the supper.

The arrival of food caused a bit of a shift round and Sarah, having lost James in the crush, found herself elbow to elbow with Rory. 'I'm glad to see you're taking my advice and getting out a bit,' he said, just as he might have to a depressed and house-bound patient.

'I don't know about that. What I do remember is you telling me that I needed a man,' she said baldly.

Rory claimed not to remember that. 'Did I really? How very forward of me! I'd not recommend James

Tait, though. You know what they say about sailors and a girl in every port.'

Sarah was smarting because Rory hadn't remembered every word he'd said to her. 'I also know the one about the doctor with a girl in every hospital,' she retorted.

That went straight over his head like water off the proverbial duck's back. 'Speaking personally,' he answered, 'I've always thought it sensible to have a good look round and weigh up the possibilities. Settling for the first girl to come along is just asking for trouble.'

Substitute 'man' for 'girl' and he could have been getting at me again, thought Sarah grimly, but she made herself smile approvingly. 'How very sensible,' she purred. 'And, of course, the longer you wait, the more chance there is of finding a girl who can help your career along, too!'

Had that been too obvious? If it had, Rory wasn't letting on. 'I certainly wouldn't want somebody who would harm it,' he retorted. Then he asked, 'Do you really want all that curried stuff? You'll be sorry in the morning!'

Sarah had been too intent on what he was saying to notice what she was putting on her plate. 'Blast!' she muttered, cross with herself as much as with him.

Rory took the plate out of her hand and swept most of the contents back in the bowl. Then he chose a more balanced selection and handed it back to her.

'Thank you,' Sarah said weakly, while wondering why it was that she could hold her own with just about anybody but him.

Rory himself had gone for simplicity with cold ham, pickles and bread. 'I hate eating standing up,' he said. 'Let's go outside and sit on the stairs.'

Sarah had noticed the little blonde sending murderous glances her way. 'But will your friend not be offended?' she asked.

'Was that friend or friends?' Rory asked innocently. 'Still, not to worry. I'll get round them all before the night's out. But perhaps you're hankering after James.'

James, as Rory could surely see, was now intent on charming the girl who'd come with Rory's blonde friend. 'Better the devil I know than the one I don't,' said Sarah.

'Very wise,' he said approvingly, carving a way through the crowd.

It was quiet on the stairs, and cooler, too. Sarah sat on the top step, with Rory two down, resting a broad shoulder against her right thigh. She could feel the warmth of him through the thin stuff of her dress and wished he didn't have this power to disturb her so much. It had always been a one-way process in the past and she had absolutely no reason to suppose things would ever be any different.

'How's Moira?' she asked abruptly.

He looked at her, his eyebrows raised. 'Moira? All right, I guess. I haven't seen her for a bit.'

How long was a 'bit'? 'I'd expected to see her here tonight,' pursued Sarah.

'Why?' asked Rory. 'She's not particularly friendly with either Robin or Carrie—or had you forgotten?'

'Not exactly…but I have been away nearly four

years. And people can change quite a lot in that time.'

He looked up at her again, his brown eyes searching. 'And how much have you changed, Sarah?' he asked quietly.

'Oh, as much as anyone else, I suppose,' she hedged. 'After all, we're all getting older. Wiser, too. At least it's to be hoped so.'

'Does that include you?'

'Why not?' she asked with a shrug.

Rory was quiet for a long moment before asking bluntly, 'What really happened? Did Steve walk out on you?'

Sarah glared at him. 'No man has ever walked out on me,' she retorted with truth, 'and I hope I'd always have the wit to walk first. If you must know, the relationship was going nowhere—and neither was my career. So I decided to come back to Britain. Simple.'

'If you say so,' said Rory slowly, 'but I'd have thought that ending something like that would have been anything but simple.'

Of course he was right—it hadn't been simple. How could ending any affair of four years' duration be simple, even when your heart had never really been in it. How was she to regain lost ground? 'What I really meant was...I gave you a simple explanation of what happened. You don't want to hear all the details. Much too boring.'

'That depends,' he said thoughtfully.

'On what?' she asked.

'On whether it would help to talk. It's not good to bottle things up, you know.'

The most important thing Sarah had got bottled

up was the way she'd always felt about him—and she certainly wasn't going to talk to him about that! He had quite enough women yearning after him as it was. 'Thanks for the offer,' she returned, 'but I'm not going to bend your ear with my troubles. Especially as they're all in the past and all resolved.' She'd nearly added 'and no harm done', but that wouldn't have been true. Career-wise, anyway.

'He hurt you, though,' Rory persisted.

Now what was he trying to do? Get her crying on his shoulder so that he could say he'd told her so? No way! Besides, that was physically impossible, given the way they were sitting.

'No more than I hurt him,' Sarah insisted. 'Not so much, actually.' By walking out on Steve, she'd left him penniless!

'Because you were the one to walk.'

'Is that not what I said?'

Her tone had been more acid than she'd realised and Rory said quietly, 'I was only trying to help, Sarah.'

'If you really mean that, then the best thing you can do is to say no more about it,' she replied in a softer tone. 'Now let's have our supper. I for one am rather hungry.'

When they returned to the party, the only person who appeared to have noticed their absence was the little blonde girl James had pointed out to Sarah earlier. She was at Rory's side in a flash, clinging to his arm and demanding, 'Where have you been? I thought for sure you must have been called away.' With that went a withering glance for Sarah.

'Just catching up,' Rory told her easily. 'Sarah

and I are old friends. Sarah Sinclair—Dulcie Carlisle. Dulcie is a nurse at the City.'

'And I suppose you're a doctor,' Dulcie said dismissively.

Sarah nodded, while Rory explained that they'd trained together.

'My father doesn't approve of women doing medicine,' declared Dulcie. 'He says it makes them hard and bossy and unfeminine.'

'Some male doctors do think like that, though fortunately my father didn't,' Sarah contrived neatly. 'He also believed that those who did were afraid of the competition.'

'Perhaps you don't know that my father is Professor of Orthopaedic Surgery in this city!'

'Really? Well, I'm not surprised. I remember Dad saying once that Graham Carlisle would go far.'

'And how far has your father got?' Dulcie asked disdainfully.

'He was killed ten years ago by a rockfall in Glen Coe, while attending to a climber trapped on a ledge,' Sarah told her quietly.

That left Dulcie with a red face and nothing to say. She still had Rory firmly under arrest, though, so Sarah slipped through a gap in the crowd and took their empty plates to the kitchen, where Fiona had already started on the clearing-up.

'I saw you and Rory sneaking out earlier,' she said as she rinsed plates, before putting them in the dishwasher. 'Don't tell me you've fallen out already!'

'You make it sound as though we spent all our time quarrelling in days gone by,' protested Sarah. There'd always been a lot of banter between them, and certainly a lot of chemistry, but nothing else. Until the day he'd found out she was going away with Steve. Sarah changed the subject by saying, 'You were kept so busy at the reunion that we didn't get the chance to talk. So, for starters, tell me where you're working these days.'

Fiona had taken up medicine with the one aim of helping the poor and needy, so Sarah wasn't in the least surprised when Fiona said she was in general practice in one of the most deprived areas of Glasgow. 'It's tough going,' she admitted, 'but very rewarding. How are you liking the Allanbank, Sarah? It must be a bonus, having Rory there.'

'I hardly ever see him,' Sarah admitted. 'And from what I hear, his spare time is, well, taken care of.'

'I'm sure you will—see more of him, I mean,' Fiona said earnestly. 'I know he's ever so pleased that you've come home.'

What a gem she was! Always helpful, always ready to say and do the right, the comforting thing. 'Perhaps, perhaps not,' said Sarah. 'What I'd really like would be for us to meet sometimes.'

Fiona was visibly pleased. 'I'd love that, Sarah. I missed you, you know. So did Carrie.' She gave a most uncharacteristic giggle. 'Do you remember all the fun we had in that awful flat of hers?' Reminiscences about their student days took them happily through the washing-up.

When they returned to the living room afterwards, most of the guests had gone. Only Angus Forbes and his wife remained chatting with Carrie and Robin and—as Angus said—helping to finish the wine. Rory must have left with the clinging Dulcie, and Sarah felt a stab of disappointment.

Carrie leapt up with a squeal. 'I thought you two had gone,' she cried. 'Don't tell me you've been doing the dishes.' She uncurled herself from her beloved and dashed over to a side table to fill two more glasses, just as the entry phone sounded.

Robin went to press the release button and came back a minute later with Rory.

He came straight over to Sarah and explained, 'Dulcie came with a friend who went off with James, leaving the poor girl stranded. So I took her home.'

'You seem to be making a career of it,' remarked Sarah.

'A career of what?'

'Taking home stranded females. I haven't forgotten your kind rescue of me after the reunion.'

He smiled briefly at the way she'd described that, before offering, 'I'll see you home tonight, if you like.'

'There's no need,' Sarah told him rather regretfully. 'I'm staying at Bruce's again—and he only lives across the road, if you remember.'

Rory smiled crookedly. 'A lot can happen, crossing a road—as I should know in my job. Still…' He turned away and sat down beside Fiona, who looked startled but pleased. She'd always had a soft spot for him, remembered Sarah. Was there no end to his options?

'How's the new job going?' asked Angus at Sarah's elbow.

'It's fine, thanks,' she told him. 'Of course, it's

only a locum, but I'm getting some very good and
varied experience.'

'And will certainly count as a plus if you do decide to take the GP course. Don't forget what I said
to you about a job, will you?' he went on. 'Dad will
be retiring in a year or two.'

'Thanks, Angus—that's really kind of you, but I
haven't made up my mind yet.'

'You're still hankering after a hospital career,' he
surmised. 'The trouble is, you've kind of dropped
behind in that race.'

Sarah answered with a sigh that she realised that,
which was why she'd sent off for the prospectus of
the GP course. It was only sensible not to turn down
the chance he was offering.

The party broke up soon afterwards. Fiona was
driving herself, while Angus and his wife were staying overnight at a nearby hotel. 'We like to give
ourselves a taste of the bright lights every now and
again,' he explained as they set off to walk.

That left Sarah and Rory standing together on the
pavement. 'I like Angus' wife,' he said firmly.

'Yes, I took to her, too,' Sarah agreed mildly.

'I'm not sure that was mutual,' said Rory, 'but,
then, she's such a gentle, timid, wee thing and rather
short on self-confidence.'

'So what are you telling me now?' asked Sarah,
her mind going back to the reunion dinner, when
he'd made a point of telling her that Angus was
married.

'Only that she adores him and is terrified of losing
him.'

Sarah gave a little chuckle. 'Surely you're not
suggesting that I could be a threat?'

'I suspect that Chrissie thinks so.'

'Rubbish!'

'It is not rubbish, Sarah. Angus makes no secret of his liking for you—and have you looked in your mirror lately?'

Sarah was getting quite exasperated with him. 'What has my mirror got to do with anything?' she demanded crisply.

'A quick glance would soon tell you why you've got wee Chrissie Forbes running scared.'

'What absolute rubbish!' Sarah told him scornfully. 'Especially coming from the one who once said I'd never muscle in and ruin anybody's life! I'm going to say goodnight now, Rory, before I get really cross!' And she started off across the road.

When she looked back, Rory had gone. I'll never figure out the way he thinks, she thought with a sigh.

All the same, while brushing her hair later, she took Rory's advice and took a good look at herself. She saw a clear-skinned oval face with full soft lips, a small straight nose, finely arched brows over large, thoughtful, dark blue eyes...

Chrissie Forbes was sweetly unexceptional while she, Sarah, was—what? Disdainfully cool, yet very appealing, Steve had told her once, but he'd never wanted to paint her.

And Rory could never have thought her up to much in the charm stakes, or why did he chase after every female but her?

There was only one answer to that. With a muttered exclamation, Sarah threw down her brush, sprang into bed and put out the light. But it was some time before she managed to sleep.

*   *   *

On returning to work on Monday morning, Sarah discovered that three more patients had been hit by stomach upsets. It was still confined to the women's ward, though, and they were hoping to keep it that way. All the same, the problem was considered serious enough to bring Miss Coull out of her office.

'I blame all this foreign travel,' she told Sarah, who'd already heard from Sister Gordon that the UNO never went further than Rothesay for her holidays. 'God knows what they pick up and bring back. That Mrs Aitken, now. She's not long back from a Mediterranean cruise.'

'She's one of the most recent victims, though,' Sarah pointed out, 'so I don't think we can blame her.'

'All the same, you'd better ring Orthopaedics and cancel that consultation for the time being.'

'I intend to,' Sarah answered crisply. 'The last thing she's needing at the moment is to have that knee examined—something that's bound to be painful—in between her trips to the loo.'

'Are you trying to teach me my job?' That was the next question for Sarah, angrily put.

'Only if you're trying to teach me mine,' Sarah returned serenely.

Miss Coull tried another tack. 'You've been abroad for several years yourself, have you not, Doctor?'

Heaven knew what she was suggesting now! Sarah decided to go for humour. 'That's quite true, Miss Coull, but as I've been back in this country for two months now, I don't think I can be the cause of this outbreak. Now, if you'll excuse me, I have an outpatient clinic looming and a phone call to make first.'

When Sarah phoned Orthopaedics from the nurses' station to explain about Mrs Aitken, it was Rory who answered.

The unsatisfactory way they'd parted two nights previously was still vivid in Sarah's mind. 'This call concerns our patient, Mrs Aitken,' she began stiffly. 'She has now developed gastroenteritis, so the consultation we requested with a view to joint replacement is no longer of immediate importance.'

'I see. Well, thank you for letting us know.' There was a slight pause during which Sarah almost put down the phone before Rory asked, 'And your own health, Doctor? What are you taking for that?'

'I— My *what*? I don't have a health problem,' she protested, totally at sea.

'I wouldn't say that,' Rory refuted smoothly. 'Paper is not easily digested.'

'What the hell are you getting at *now*?' asked Sarah, causing considerable interest among the staff within earshot.

'The fact that you've obviously swallowed a dictionary. You must have quite a tummy-ache yourself after that—or, as you'd probably put it, be experiencing considerable gastric discomfort.'

'Oh, go to blazes!' she growled, before slamming down the phone. 'Just talking to an old friend,' she explained to the listeners, which only served to fuel their curiosity.

Sarah had always been able to switch off from her personal problems in order to concentrate one hundred per cent on her patients, so Rory and his mysterious attitude towards her would be banished to the back of her mind for the next two hours. She enjoyed her clinics. Of course, the most difficult and obscure cases went to the consultant but, with the registrar absent so often, Sarah was getting plenty of chances to exercise her diagnostic skills.

Most of them were regulars this morning, and one such was a Mr Hamish McWhirter. Her heart sank as he shuffled in with his Zimmer. She got up to settle him safely on the patient's chair, before asking, 'What happened to your sticks, Mr McWhirter? I thought we'd agreed they'd be more convenient about the house and so on than this thing.' She put the Zimmer to one side.

'Aye, lass, right enough, but the Zimmer gets us more sympathy, ken? So I gave the sticks to ma neighbour. He'd run out of canes for his garden.'

'That was very naughty of you,' chided Sarah, striving to keep calm. 'The NHS wasn't set up to supply garden equipment, you know.'

'Eh? Oh, I get it—very funny, Doctor,' he wheezed appreciatively. 'What a lassie.'

'How's the asthma?' asked Sarah, who knew when she was licked.

'Well, now, I'm not rightly sure it is asthma,' he argued, and he was right. That was a diagnosis he'd made himself at his last visit.

'So you agree with me now that it's the cigarettes to blame?' she asked hopefully.

'Ach, no! I'm immune to them like ma dad and his dad. I telt ye that!' He leaned forward confidingly. 'I've narrowed it down to the wool.'

'The wool,' repeated Sarah, sounding quite dazed.

'Aye, you know, yon stuff the auld woman uses. For the knitting. At it day and night she is—clack,

clack, clack wi' yon steel needles till ye cannae hear the racin' on the telly. If ye could jest mebbe have a word—tell her she's makin' us ill...'

'You want me to tell your wife that her knitting wool is bad for your chest?'

'Aye, that's right.'

'Supposing I were to tell you that your non-stop smoking is giving her bronchitis?'

'Och away! How could that be?'

'It's much more likely than your notion that her knitting wool is giving you a bad chest. Now, then, Mr McWhirter! I have here a list of all the advice I've given you over the weeks. If you refuse to face up to things then that's your choice, but don't blame me or the hospital or your family doctor if your health continues to get worse. You've got nobody to blame but yourself.'

He was quiet for so long that Sarah thought she'd really got through to him this time. Then he said, 'Talkin' o' health, Doctor, them pains in ma legs is no better. Ma own doctor says the blood supply's likely goin'. Why would that be?'

'The nicotine in the cigarettes is hardening the arteries—something else I've told you more than once.'

There was another second or two of silence before he said, 'I saw a great wee buggy thing the other day—like a wee car, it was. Electric. Just great for gettin' to the shops and that. Could you get me one like that, now ma legs is sae bad?'

Talk about ostriches burying their heads in sand! They had nothing on Hamish McWhirter. 'The answer is no,' Sarah said firmly. 'And the sooner you wake up to the fact that nothing mechanical can possibly be better than your own two legs, the better. Stop smoking and your bronchitis will improve. So will the pain in your legs. So will your wife's chest. It's all up to you.'

'Aye, ye're a great one for the speeches, Doctor,' he said admiringly. 'Ye should be standin' for the parliament, ye're that good at it.' he reached for his walking aid and lumbered to his feet. 'I've telt ye and telt ye, Doctor. It's no' the ciggies 'cos us McWhirters is immune. It's sheep. I cannae eat lamb neither. Gives us terrible pains. Another month, eh?' And away he went, leaving Sarah unsure whether to scream, cry or laugh at the sheer absurdity of the man.

He was only the first of many patients she had to see that morning, so she settled for clenching her fists and exhaling loudly. Then she buzzed for the next one.

But Hamish McWhirter and his silliness stayed with her all morning, and she was puzzling over the best line to take with him all the way to the canteen. In the doorway, she almost collided with Rory and his sidekick, Peter Blair. 'You look as though you had the weight of the world on your shoulders,' Rory told her. 'Lighten up, girl. It may never happen.'

'I'm only too certain that it will,' she said with a sigh, before giving them a potted version of her session with Mr McWhirter. 'What would you do?' she appealed.

Rory scratched his nose thoughtfully. 'You could try showing him some grisly pictures of a gangrenous foot. I knew a consultant who did that—and it worked. But it sounds to me as though this patient of yours is too complete a nicotine addict,' he went on gloomily.

'You're a great help,' said Sarah.

'Well, you know me. Always ready to help a pal.' He stroked her cheek softly, before advising, 'Cheer up, love. You've obviously given it your best shot and nobody could do more. The rest is up to him.'

He turned away when his consultant came along to claim his attention and Peter said with a grin, 'Anybody who wasn't in the know would think you two were an old married couple the way you talk to one another.'

Sarah's heart sank, because that was exactly how it was and always had been. Why had she never realised? Because she didn't want to, of course!

'I know,' she admitted at last with a catch in her breath.

CHAPTER FOUR

MISS COULL intercepted Sarah next morning before she could get the length of Sister Gordon's office. 'We have two more cases of gastroenteritis, Dr Sinclair.'

'Oh, dear.'

'Exactly. And none of the others are any better.'

'Still, it's something that it's confined to one ward.' Sarah knew that, having already done her round of the men.

'So far,' Miss Coull replied in doom-laden tones. 'And now you'll have to excuse me, Doctor. I'm expecting an important visitor from the Royal College of Nursing. The new cases are Buchan and Scott.' She made them sound more like a firm of solicitors than two ailing women.

'Is Sister Gordon off duty today?' Sarah asked of a retreating back.

Miss Coull turned round, looking puzzled. 'No—why?'

'I thought she must be—as you're here.'

'I am always available in emergencies,' Sarah was told.

Except on the men's side, thought Sarah with a secret smile. It was whispered that the UNO was terrified of Jack Kinnear—simply because he was a man.

Mrs Buchan was indeed showing symptoms of gastric upset, but when Miss Scott confessed to eat-

ing a whole basket of fruit the night before, Sarah
decided to reserve judgment. Despite Miss Coull's
gloomy view of things, the disease was following
its normal course in the others and Sarah thought
that another twenty-four hours would see the end of
it.

She cadged a quick coffee from Jack Kinnear and
then it was down to Outpatients for a clinic. Nobody
that morning came anywhere near Hamish
McWhirter for cussedness and one o'clock found
Sarah heading for lunch in the canteen.

She met Rory coming out. 'Why, Sarah,' he said,
looking quite pleased to see her, 'this saves me giving you a ring. Are you going to Professor Wood's
lecture at the institute tonight? If so, I could give
you a lift.'

'Thanks, but I can't. I'm on call.'

His smile faded at the abruptness of her reply, but
he said easily enough, 'That's a pity—the old boy
is always well worth listening to. Even if his spe-
ciality is not yours.' Professor Wood was a byword
in psychology.

'I'm sure.' Sarah was struggling with a tongue-
tied feeling. 'It was a kind thought. Some other time
perhaps?'

'Why not?' he said neutrally. 'See you around,
then—perhaps.'

It had been only a brief exchange, but quite
enough to take the shine off a day that hadn't been
going all that well anyway. I've simply got to
lighten up with him, she told herself as she collected
a plate of mince and potatoes. If I go on like this,
I'll not even have him for a friend.

'Sarah! Glad I caught you!' It was Bill Ferguson,

her opposite number on Geriatrics. He dropped into the chair beside her. 'I suppose you couldn't possibly swop on-call with me this week, could you? Something's come up.'

'You want me to do tomorrow instead of tonight,' she guessed.

'You've got it. Of course, if you've got a heavy date yourself tomorrow, then—'

'Nothing special,' said Sarah. Nothing at all, she thought. 'OK, I'll swop, Bill. It makes no difference to me.'

'You're an angel,' he declared. 'Did anybody ever tell you that?'

'Often—when wanting a favour,' she said wryly. 'Oh, get along with you! Who knows? I might want a favour from you one day.' Her mind was already busy with a promising scenario. Now she could go with Rory to that lecture and perhaps improve things. Quite what she meant by that, Sarah wasn't sure.

It was mid-afternoon before she found time to ring Rory and ask for the proffered lift. She was told that Dr Drummond was in Theatre and couldn't be disturbed.

'But presumably he'll be coming up to the wards afterwards,' she persisted, 'so would you please tell him that Dr Sinclair from Dr Marshall's unit needs to speak to him urgently?'

That provoked a muffled chuckle at the other end of the line. 'Surely, Doctor, I'll add your name to the list.' Sarah found the reply irritating. Wretched female thinks I'm smitten with him, she thought. But, then, she was, wasn't she? Had it shown in her voice?

A last-minute emergency, which turned out to be nothing more than too heavy a lunch, meant that Sarah was late going off duty. There had been no return call from Rory, so she'd have to hurry if she was to get to the medical institute on time.

She arrived at the lecture hall just as they were shutting the doors and had to make do with a stool, brought most unwillingly, set down behind a pillar at the back. Before the questions afterwards, Sarah stood up and peered round, hoping to see Rory, but it was no good. The hall was very large, it was packed to the doors and the light was too poor to recognise anyone more than fifteen feet away.

Afterwards, when Sarah was waiting at the bus stop, Rory came along with Moira and several other people she didn't recognise. He stared at her, then dropped back behind his companions and demanded, 'Were you at that lecture?'

'Yes. I—I managed to change duties,' she stammered, feeling absurdly nervous, sensing that he didn't believe her.

'Catch you up in a minute,' he said, when Moira turned round curiously. 'It's all right—I got the message,' he told Sarah in a harsh unfriendly voice. 'I'm only sorry you felt you had to lie to get it across.' Then he hurried after the others.

'Rory, no, I...' But the right words wouldn't come and she was left to watch the possessive way Moira thrust her arm through Rory's and her dismissive backward glance before the whole party turned into a brightly lit restaurant.

Sarah was puzzled and quite miserable and wished she hadn't bothered to go to the lecture. It was clear that whoever had taken her message that afternoon hadn't passed it on. Was Rory angry because he thought she'd refused his offer of a lift because she didn't want to go with him? She could try telling him how she'd tried to get in touch, but would he believe her?

'Are ye wantin' this bus, hen?'

Sarah came to herself and realised that she was holding up the queue. 'Um, yes, sorry...' She climbed aboard, slipped some coins in the box and took the nearest seat without collecting her ticket. She resumed her thinking. Why had Rory seemed so offended? She puzzled over that all the way back to the hospital, coming up with a most unsatisfactory answer. She hadn't been exactly charming since they'd met again. Now he was fed up with her and had taken the first chance that offered to drop the old pals act. She'd asked for this and, knowing it, only made it worse.

By the time the bus screeched to a halt at the hospital gates it was raining hard and Sarah wasn't wearing a mac. The staff quarters were about as far from the gate as they could be, and by the time she got under cover she was soaked. And when she went for a hot bath, the water was tepid.

My next job is going to be in a hot country and at least ten miles from the nearest man, she vowed idiotically as she climbed, shivering, into bed.

Despite Miss Coull's gloomy predictions, most of the gastric patients had almost recovered by the next day. 'But if you sneeze all over them like this, Doctor, there's no telling where it'll all end,' she said with a sigh.

'Would you like me to wear a mask in the wards,

then?' asked Sarah, rather spoiling the effect with
another sneeze.

'I think, on the whole, no. An infectious doctor
could alarm a nervous patient.' Nobody had ever
been known to get the better of Miss Coull. Must
be something to do with her peculiar reasoning,
thought Sarah.

Halfway through the afternoon, Mrs Aitken—the
patient with the very bad knee and the penchant for
foreign cruises—got up too quickly to pour a drink
for her neighbour in the next bed, lost her footing
and slid under the bed. The nearest nurse alerted
Sarah, who rang Orthopaedics and asked to speak to
Dr Blair.

'Mrs Aitken,' he said. 'Would that be the little
lady we were asked to see with a view to knee replacement?'

'Got it in one, Pete. Unfortunately, she's just
taken a bit of a tumble and given it a nasty wrench.
Could you possibly come and check her over for
me, please? I'd welcome an expert opinion.'

'What a flatterer.' He laughed. 'Would half an
hour's time do?'

Sarah thanked him and went back to work.

It was Rory, not Peter, who came. He was cool,
efficient and completely switched off, which left
Sarah with no alternative but to act the same way.

'This is really very good of you,' she said for-
mally.

He eyed her stonily and said, 'I'd rather thought
I was just doing my job. After all, your consultant
did ask for an opinion, and mine has decided I'm
competent to assess her for replacement at the
same time.

'I don't think she's done any serious damage,' he said, after looking at the knee, 'but a replacement is definitely in order sooner rather than later. We'll be in touch. You were quite right to alert us,' he ended, as though speaking to a green junior.

'Thank you *so* much,' returned Sarah to his retreating back. She was hurting inside. Only now, when it had all gone wrong, was she realising how much she'd been hoping that she and Rory would finally have found themselves on the same wavelength. Still, she'd soon be away from this hospital and not be looking for him all the time. But that was no comfort at all.

Next morning, while Sarah was helping with the routine blood samples, a nurse came to tell her that she was wanted on the phone. 'Ask if you can take a message, please,' said Sarah. 'I must get these done before the morning collection.'

When the nurse didn't return, Sarah assumed it hadn't been anything important and carried on with her tedious task, thinking what a bonus it would be when the houseman had learned to speed up and free her for her own tasks.

There were more than enough of those today. Two patients were going home and she had to see their relatives to talk about care and assistance for the foreseeable future. Dr Marshall insisted on these personal briefings as too often patients give their nearest and dearest quite the wrong idea of their problems and needs.

Not long before going off duty that night, Sarah discovered a memo on her desk, underneath her mail.

'Mr Drummond rang. No message,' it read.

Sarah took it along to the nurses' station to ask if anyone knew how long it had been there. One of the girls took it and said, 'That's Tracy's writing and she went off duty at two, so it must have come before that. Would it be something to do with Mrs Aitken, Doctor?'

'Almost certainly,' decided Sarah. 'Just so long as I've not overlooked anything.'

'Not you, Dr Sinclair. You're always on the ball, despite what Miss Coull says.'

Sarah thanked her for that. It had been a back-handed compliment, but still worth having. The phone on her desk was ringing when she got back to the doctors' room. She picked it up and said, 'Dr Sinclair speaking.'

'Sarah—it's Rory.' He sounded awkward and ill at ease. 'About that call of yours. Was there a problem, or has it been resolved?'

'What call?' she asked. 'I've not rung Orthopaedics since yesterday. About Mrs Aitken. You came to see her if you—'

'Not that one—the one on Tuesday afternoon. This morning I found a note on my desk under a pile of case notes. It says, ''Dr Sinclair rang this afternoon and says she needs to speak to you urgently.'' I'm just apologising for the oversight—presumably, whatever the problem was, it's now resolved.'

'You could say that,' Sarah agreed quietly. 'It was after I'd switched on-call with Bill Ferguson—at his request. Being suddenly free, I thought I may as well go to Professor Wood's lecture, so I rang to ask if the lift was still on offer—that's all.'

There was quite a pause before Rory asked in quite a different tone, 'What are you doing now, Sarah?'

'I was just about to go off duty when you rang.'

'There's a small hotel called the Weavers' Arms about fifty yards down the road from the hospital and on the other side of the road. Do you know it?'

She could hardly speak for hope. 'I've seen it from the bus...'

'Will you meet me there in about an hour?' he asked in a rush.

She forced herself to say lightly, 'Sure. Why not?'

'Good! See you there, then.' He hung up.

Sarah almost ran to her room. She was as excited as a teenager before her first date. I must keep my sense of proportion, she warned herself as she showered and dressed. This is nothing more than a drink after work with an old friend. But sensible thoughts like that didn't stop her putting on a pretty patterned skirt with a scoop-necked black blouse and a necklace of Venetian glass beads.

Sarah got to the hotel first. She had left her long black hair loose and it shone from much brushing. Her blue eyes shone with anticipation, which could be why they asked if she was a guest at the birthday party.

'No—just meeting a colleague for a drink,' she answered, so they put her to wait in the cocktail lounge.

Rory was so late that Sarah had begun to wonder if she should leave. 'God, I'm so sorry,' he apologised, dropping down on the bench beside her. 'A last-minute hold-up—but you know all about those.' He eyed her with something that could have been approval and said, 'You're looking very nice. Almost good enough for a ball. Are you going on somewhere?'

Sarah felt a small stab of doubt. 'No, I...no,' she faltered as Rory asked, looking at her empty glass. 'Can I get you another of those?'

'Is there time?' she asked. 'If you're late for something...having been delayed.'

'I'm not going on anywhere either,' he said, then he ordered her another spritzer and a half of lager for himself.

'You're very abstemious these days,' said Sarah when she heard that. Rory had never been a heavy drinker, but at least that was something to say.

He smiled briefly and said, 'Could be I feel I need a clear head for the matter in hand.'

'And what would that be?' she asked, with another stab of doubt.

After an almost unbearable pause he said, 'We seem to have got our wires crossed, Sarah. What do you say to having a go at uncrossing them?'

'I say it's a good idea,' she answered.

'You've changed,' he said, apparently going off at a tangent.

'In what way?' she asked guardedly. Her euphoria over this meeting had all but evaporated.

'You don't talk so much, for one thing.'

Her lips twisted in a wry little smile. 'Surely you're not complaining? There was a time when you thought I talked far too much.'

'There is a middle way,' said Rory.

Would he never get to the point—whatever it was? 'Crossed wires,' she reminded him. 'We were going to try a spot of unravelling.'

He sipped his drink, looking over her shoulder and avoiding her eyes. His own were wary. 'Tuesday,' he said eventually. 'When you said you couldn't go to that lecture—and then turned up—I thought you were telling me to drop the old mate act and get lost.'

'Oh, Rory, really!' She'd never have believed that anybody with his self-possession could possibly have thought like that. 'I knew I'd been kind of reserved and cagey with everybody since I came home, so when you said you'd got the message, and so on, I thought that you'd…run out of patience with me when you were only trying to be friendly.'

'You *do* understand,' he said as his face relaxed in a broad grin. 'We were always such good friends, were we not? And after you went away, I, well, I really missed you. And as far as I'm concerned, it'd be just great if we could get back on the old footing.'

Was half a loaf really better than no bread? In these circumstances, Sarah decided that it was.

'We always went Dutch,' she recalled, 'so now it's my turn to get them in.'

'I've got a better idea,' said Rory. 'There's nothing in my fridge but eggs, but I can't believe you'd rather have supper in the canteen, so why don't we eat here? I'm told they do very good steaks.'

'Sounds like a good idea to me.' Sarah smiled, taking her cue from him, just nice and casual.

An hour later and it was almost like old times. Rory was totally at ease and clearly enjoying himself. Sarah was enjoying her evening, too, but perhaps not quite so much. In the old days, she'd lived in the hope of her love one day being returned. Now she knew there was no hope of that. Only half a loaf, Sarah. But for the past four years she'd not even had that.

When they were on their third coffees, Rory asked Sarah if she'd got anything lined up for when her locum job finished.

'Before I came here, I applied for a registrarship in Portsmouth.'

Rory gasped.

'Yes, I know,' said Sarah, sure that she knew the cause of that gasp. 'A bit over-optimistic, with only fifteen months work in this country on offer—and, of course, I wasn't even short-listed. My mother and sister want me to try for something near them, in Surrey.'

Rory was frowning heavily. 'I don't think that's a good idea at all,' he declared firmly. 'You'll stand a much better chance of advancement here in Glasgow. Gold medallists aren't easily forgotten, so why not give the Dean a ring? You must remember how much he likes giving advice.'

'I might do that,' agreed Sarah, the thought not having occurred to her. 'On the other hand, I could sign up for the next GP course.'

'You always said you wanted a hospital career!'

'I know, but we can't always have what we want,' said an older and wiser Sarah.

'You can say that again!' Rory fervently agreed.

'When did you ever miss out on anything you wanted, Rory Drummond?' she asked incredulously.

'Don't you go thinking my life's been all a bed of roses, my girl!'

'Oh, come on! You always knew exactly what you wanted!' To be a consultant orthopaedic surgeon—an ambition he was right on course to achieve.

'Not always,' he denied. 'Sometimes...' He was having to search for words again and that wasn't like him at all. He made up his mind and said, 'There was...something I wanted, only I didn't realise until it was too late... Och, well, we're all the same when we're young,' he went on more lightly. 'Before we learn to compromise.'

'That's certainly what I'll be doing if I settle for general practice.'

'Promise me you'll not do anything until you've spoken to the Dean,' he begged earnestly.

'All right,' agreed Sarah. 'It can't do any harm.'

'That's the spirit—and now I think we'll have to move before they throw us out.' They were the only people left in the lounge and lights were dimming here and there. 'This has been such a good evening, Sarah, that I'd quite lost track of time.'

He walked back with her to the staff quarters and on the doorstep he laid his hands on her shoulders. 'Friends again?' he asked.

'Friends, Rory.'

'I'll hold you to that,' he told her positively, increasing the pressure of his hands for a second.

But he'd made no mention of another meeting like this, she thought with disappointment as he strode away towards the staff car park.

'Message for you from Dr Gray,' said Charge Nurse Jack Kinnear when Sarah walked into his office next morning. 'Can you stand by to finish her clinic this afternoon? She has to leave early.'

'Well, fancy that—and on a Friday, too,' returned

Sarah, who was rapidly running out of patience with the registrar.

'You're a terrible cynic for such a lovely girl,' teased Jack, 'but it's not a hairdresser's appointment today. She's got an appointment with her obstetrician.'

'Much more of this place and I'll be making an appointment with a psychiatrist,' Sarah said, sighing. 'And it's my weekend on, too. Still, with luck this will be the last but one.'

'This unit will fall apart when you leave,' said Jack, only half in jest.

'Not while you're here, it won't! Any particular problems among your boys today, Jack?'

'Only with that peppery old ex-army chap who came in on Wednesday, but nobody's come up with a cure for bad temper yet.'

Things went smoothly for once that morning until Sarah went to assist the registrar with a bronchoscopy. Then, having extracted a specimen from the lung of their sedated patient, Dr Gray came over faint and left Sarah to finish off, write the appropriate request form and send the suspect tissue sample to the path lab. Sarah decided to deliver it herself on her way to lunch.

The queue in the canteen was as long as she'd ever seen it, but she cheered up on seeing Rory a little way ahead. When he caught sight of Sarah, he dropped back to join her. 'I was going to ring you,' he said, cheering her up even more. 'About a patient,' he added, damping down her elation.

It was a familiar story. A pleasant old man in his late seventies had been doing really well after his hip replacement until he'd had a recurrence of a

chronic respiratory complaint for which Dr Marshall
had had him under review for several years.

'So there you have it,' said Rory. 'He's not fit for
discharge, but his bed is already promised to another
patient. Could you not take him over for us, Sarah?
A little bird told me you've got a bed.'

'Only for this morning—we're admitting another
patient just about now. Is he really not well enough
to go home, Rory?'

'He would be, if he didn't live alone. Do your
best for us, Sarah.'

'Short of putting them two in a bed, I don't see
what I can do,' she returned. 'You know, what's
really needed is a sort of halfway house somewhere
in the grounds. There's plenty of room.'

Rory smiled at such naïvety. 'Pie in the sky,
Sarah. And even if it did get off the ground, it'd be
just like opening a new road. Bliss for a week and
gridlock in a month.'

'It's not right that we should be so continually
pressed for beds like this!' she declared hotly.

'I couldn't agree more,' he said, 'but with so
many acute beds—medical and surgical—filled with
patients suffering from serious self-induced illness,
or carelessness of some sort, what can be done?
Life-threatening conditions—no matter how they are
induced—get priority.'

'Too true,' she agreed. 'I wonder if I should take
up preventative medicine?'

'On days like this, I'm inclined to think I'd be
better off working in a zoo,' said Rory with a sigh.
'Nobody objects to money going into animal care.

'I enjoyed last night,' he said offhandedly when
they were seated at last.

'So did I. I've not tasted a steak like that for years.'

'I thought the company was quite good, too,' he returned pointedly.

'I wasn't suggesting—'

'I should hope not. We've declared a truce—remember?'

'I remember,' said Sarah. 'But it's my turn next time, though, huh?'

'What for?' asked Rory.

'To pick up the bill, of course, dozy.' That was just what the old Sarah would have said. I'm getting there, she thought.

Rory looked thoughtful. 'Going Dutch was all right when we were both penniless students, but I earn more than you now, so—'

'Don't remind me,' she begged. 'But you know me—always ready to pay my share.'

'We'll see,' he hedged as he sent her a questing look. 'I was thinking of going up to the Trossachs for a spot of hill-walking some Sunday soon. Care to come?'

'Rory, I would love to! Unfortunately I'm on this coming weekend, though.'

'And I'm on the one after. What a bind!'

Sarah was wishing he'd sounded even half as disappointed as she felt. 'Perhaps Moira can go with you,' she suggested, to see how he'd react.

He burst out laughing. 'Sarah, you really are a scream! Can you honestly see Moira legging it up Ben Venue in her spiky heels? No, lassie. Her idea of a good time is dinner at the latest restaurant, followed by legs up on the sofa with a glass of good wine and a video.'

He was very well informed. And did the evening end with the sofa and the video, or was there a sequel, with Moira, legs wide, somewhere else in his flat? 'How about the Sunday after the next two, then?' she asked quickly.

'That's a date,' said Rory. 'Weather permitting.'

'If it doesn't, there's always…a video.'

'True—but not nearly so healthy.'

'Let's pray for a fine day, then,' said Sarah. 'Well, I don't know about you, me ole mate, but I was due in clinic…' she looked at her watch '…three minutes ago. Let's lunch again some time.' She'd been aiming for casual but friendly. Had she got it right? How difficult it was when it mattered so much…

'Could you see Mrs Dingwall first, please, Doctor? Apparently, she fell against the cooker just before she came out, and her whole left side is badly bruised,' explained the clinic nurse the minute Sarah appeared.

'Of course,' she agreed, thinking of her earlier conversation with Rory. Once again, an accident had superceded a planned appointment.

It would have been a lengthy clinic, even without the tail end of Dr Gray's list added to Sarah's own. An even busier evening followed and then a night of broken sleep. By seven p.m. on a Saturday that saw Sarah running all over the hospital she wanted nothing more than a shower and a rest.

What she got was Rory in the residents' sitting room with a Sainsbury's take-away. 'Remembering my own days as a lowly resident, it seemed the decent thing to do,' he said in the face of her astonishment.

Sarah watched him setting out pâté, cold chicken and salad and a wicked-looking creamy dessert. He'd even brought plates and cutlery. 'Rory Drummond, I could kiss you!' she declared dreamily.

'You must be really far gone, then,' he said. 'You only ever kissed me once—and that was at the graduation ball after too much champagne.'

She looked at him hopefully and said, 'Fancy you remembering that!'

'How could I forget? You kissed every man in the party, including Fiona's second cousin who turned out to be gay. No wonder he looked like throwing up.'

'Maurice? Gay? I never guessed—but I'm a lot less innocent now,' said Sarah, spreading pâté thickly on the Melba toast Rory had also thoughtfully provided.

'Leaving aside the question of your innocence, past and present, your appetite has remained the same,' said Rory as he watched.

'I'll have you know that nothing has passed my lips since porridge and toast almost twelve hours ago,' she claimed with a wounded look.

'Seems I was just in time, then. No wonder you were nearly desperate enough to kiss me.'

'I'm so glad you understand,' Sarah said thickly, through a delicious mouthful. She had to be careful not to scare him off.

'Don't worry, I understand all right,' Rory assured her wryly.

When Sarah got a call right after the main course, she was afraid that Rory would take that as a chance to go, but he said, 'Don't mind me, hen. I'll be just fine with my feet up and the telly on.'

That brought Moira to mind again. Was it possible that he was only cultivating Sarah in order to make Moira jealous? That was a thought to bring a girl out in goose-pimples. Concentrate on work, Sarah…

It wasn't much of an emergency—just a patient who was refusing to take her sleeping pills and could be relied on to keep the rest of the ward awake if she didn't.

'Serious, was it?' asked Rory when Sarah returned to the sitting room. He was still alone, so the others on duty must have been even busier than she.

'What?' she asked.

'That call. You look as though you'd just attended a major disaster.'

Only if Moira Stirling turned out to be a major disaster… 'Oh, so-so, but I sorted it out. Rory, it's really, really good of you to give up your Saturday evening like this.'

'I never do anything unless there's something in it for me,' he claimed with a comical grin.

Sarah took that seriously, convinced now that he was using her to annoy Moira. It didn't occur to her to wonder how Moira was supposed to find out.

'If you say so. Shall I make some coffee?' Sarah crossed over to the sideboard and switched on the machine which was always on standby—like the staff. She didn't turn round until she was sure of having her face under control.

Rory had been watching Sarah with interest, but when she did turn round he was lounging back in his chair, completely at ease. 'Dessert?' he asked.

'Try and stop me! I adore any sort of pudding.'

'I remembered,' he said.

'You can be so awfully kind!'

'Wasn't I always?'

'Did I say otherwise? And very sensible of you, too, when kindness is a winner with all us girls.'

'I'll bring four courses next time, then,' he came back smartly.

'Tomorrow?' she asked before she could stop herself.

'I wish I could, but sadly I can't,' he said. He'd sounded sincere, but he didn't tell her why he couldn't see her.

Then, with the worst possible timing, two other duty doctors came in and had to be offered a share of the goodies.

The next time Sarah was called, Rory said it was getting late so he might as well go too.

'That was a truly heavenly meal, Rory—I really appreciated it,' said Sarah as they parted at the outside door.

'More or less what I intended, me dear ole mate,' he said with a smile in his voice. 'Don't work too hard now—be seeing you.'

'Have a nice day tomorrow,' called Sarah, but he didn't seem to hear her. Was it Moira's turn tomorrow—or Dulcie's?

CHAPTER FIVE

SUNDAY itself was quietish, but Sunday night was a killer so, not for the first time after a hectic night on duty, Sarah arrived on the wards on Monday morning pale and yawning.

Miss Coull wasn't amused. 'I always try to make a point of being alert at the start of the day, Doctor,' she pronounced.

Tired or not, Sarah rose to that. 'You're so right, my dear Miss Coull, but sadly that is somewhat difficult after three broken nights in a row. And last night I didn't get to my bed at all. Duty weekend,' she added, to drive home her point.

'Ah, um, yes,' replied the UNO, which was probably as near an apology as she allowed herself to get, thought Sarah.

She was shamed next minute when Miss Coull went on, 'There are no outstanding problems in my wards this morning, so perhaps you would care to join me in my office for a quick cup of coffee. I have been here since seven-thirty,' she added.

'Thank you very much,' Sarah responded weakly, never having expected to live to see this day.

'You're very late,' teased Jack Kinnear when Sarah eventually appeared on his ward.

'Only because I began my day by having coffee with my friend Miss Coull,' she boasted.

Jack's eyebrows shot skywards. 'You'd get round the devil himself,' he reckoned. 'Would it be asking too much of your Powerfulness for an opinion on a case of cellulitis?'

'I think I might oblige,' returned Sarah, laughing. 'After all, it's what I'm paid for.

'That definitely wasn't there on Saturday,' she said firmly when she saw the angry, scaly, red patch on Charlie Greig's left shin. 'It's a streptococcal infection all right. Is anybody else showing signs?'

Jack said no, and in anticipation of her diagnosis he'd already put out a warning about cross-infection.

'Good. I'll write him up for some Aureomycin and he must keep the leg elevated—in or out of bed—until it settles. And for heaven's sake, don't let him scratch it!'

Jack called her a cheeky monkey and wondered aloud if she'd like him to tie Charlie's hands to the bedpost. 'Unless you'll settle for cotton mitts,' he added.

'Just testing,' said Sarah with a smile, pretending to duck as Jack raised a playful fist.

Charlie's leg was as tricky as it got that morning, and Sarah was able to go to the canteen quite early. She was hoping to see Rory but he didn't appear, and after her second coffee it was time to go to Outpatients.

Her first patient was tragic—an eighty-year-old man with longstanding chronic bronchitis which was affecting his heart. He was also struggling to look after his even older wife who had senile dementia. Their doctor had said in the referral letter that he felt it was high time they were both in care, preferably in Allanbank Hospital's long-term wards.

On the face of it Sarah had to agree, but she changed her mind when she talked to the old man.

'If they split us up, it'll kill us, Doctor,' he pleaded with tears in his eyes. 'Sixty-one years we've been married and only parted by the War. I'm the only one she kens now. She'd go frantic without me—and I'd not get a minute's peace for worrying about her. Putting us both to sleep would be kinder.'

By then Sarah was almost in tears herself. 'I'll do my very best for you,' she promised fervently. 'Surely Social Services must see it makes more sense all round to give you the support you need in your own home, since that's what you want.'

'It is, Doctor, only the girls—our daughters—keep saying enough is enough.'

'Do they help you at all?'

'They come round when they can, only with their families and their jobs... Och, I reckon they want us in somewhere so they can stop worrying.'

Very likely, thought Sarah, but their peace of mind wasn't her problem. 'It's what *you* need that concerns me,' she answered, 'and I'll do my level best to see that you get it,' she emphasised.

The old man was so pathetically grateful that Sarah felt depressed. Supposing her efforts proved fruitless? How could she ever face him again?

As soon as the clinic was over she began her enquiries. Geriatrics promised an early appointment for assessment and suggested Social Services in the meantime. Social Services were sympathetic, but said they knew of dozens such cases and the home help service was stretched to breaking point. It was the same with the community nursing service. What about nursing homes? they suggested.

An hour later Sarah hadn't located one that would take them both—even in separate rooms. 'We try not to mix the sexes,' explained one matron. 'It's so unsettling for the others.'

'But they've been together for seventy years, for heaven's sake!' Sarah exploded, exaggerating in such a good cause.

The matron wasn't prepared to 'open the flood gates', as she put it.

'Nonsense! How many doubly disabled couples do you know?' asked Sarah, but too late. She was talking to herself.

She put a note, asking for his assistance, on Dr Marshall's desk, before going to beg some aspirin from the treatment room. What with one thing and another, she had the father and mother of a headache and she was meeting Fiona for a meal in town that night.

As she waited at the bus stop, Rory stopped his car at the kerb. 'What a bit of luck,' he said. 'When I looked at the board and saw you'd checked out, I thought to myself, well, that's that for the day. Where are you going?'

'To town. I'm meeting Fiona at that Italian place opposite the Theatre Royal.'

'Mind if I come, too?' he asked. 'I hate eating alone.'

'Sure—why not?' asked Sarah, feeling her headache subsiding as she got into the car. 'Are we not all pals together?'

She noticed his enhanced tan. 'You look as though you had a good day in the open yesterday.'

He shot her a quick glance, before admitting to quite a decent hike in the Campsies. He meant the Campsie Fells, an attractive range of low, undulating hills to the north of the city.

'Not Ben Venue? I *am* disappointed.'

'I'm saving that up for you,' he said.

'Surely you didn't go walking alone yesterday, Rory.'

'No with a few folk I know from the city,' he said vaguely.

Including the ravishing Dulcie, no doubt! Still, safety in numbers…

'What sort of a day did you have?' he asked, cutting across her thoughts.

'Fascinating,' she said. 'I am now the world's leading expert on tummy-ache, haemorrhoids, constipation and this funny feeling all over but especially down there, Doctor. And that was only in the morning!'

'Sounds a bit like general practice,' he returned, chuckling at her description.

'In that case, yesterday will stand me in good stead if I—'

'Have you not phoned the Dean yet?' he demanded.

'Listen, mate,' said Sarah firmly, 'I've been at it like a galley slave ever since agreeing to that bright idea of yours. But I'll certainly get round to it before the week's out.'

Rory parked just around the corner from the trattoria in a small yard marked PRIVATE, but to which he had a key. 'Courtesy of a grateful patient,' he explained. 'It makes a terrific difference to an evening in town.'

'I'll bet—but, then, you always did fall on your feet,' she said.

'Not always,' he corrected her.

'Give me just one instance!' she challenged.

Rory eyed her sideways, before revealing, 'This'll
have you weeping. When I was six my white mouse
died—and my granny wouldn't let me have another.'

Sarah burst out laughing. 'If that's the worst thing
that ever happened to you, then you've led a
charmed life.'

'I didn't say it was the worst thing…' He slid a
hand under Sarah's elbow to steer her through the
traffic, and the contact put everything else out of her
mind.

How was it possible for attraction like this to be
so completely one-sided? And for the unattracted
one to be so completely unaware?

Fiona was already there and had been put at a
table for two. 'Gosh!' she said when she saw Rory.

'He asked if he could come, too, and I didn't like
to say no,' explained Sarah. 'You know how sensitive he is.'

'Gosh!' repeated Fiona, who hadn't known anything of the sort.

Rory, meanwhile, had grabbed a passing waiter
who found them a bigger table.

The meal passed very pleasantly, mostly in rem-
iniscing about their student days, with none of the
awkwardness a threesome sometimes generated.
Rory insisted on treating the girls, saying it was the
least he could do, having muscled in on their party.
'Mind you, I'd have thought twice about it had it
been anywhere more pricey,' he claimed, making
them laugh some more.

Fiona said she hadn't enjoyed herself so much for
ages, which struck Sarah as rather sad. Rory said
that he hadn't either and they should do this again

very soon. Then they walked Fiona to the multi-storey car park, where she'd left her little Fiat.

'Which nights are you on this week, Sarah?' asked Rory when they'd waved Fiona out of sight.

'Only Wednesday—having been on all weekend.'

'Same with me. Is that not handy?'

'In what way?' she asked, hoping she didn't sound too eager.

'Because on Wednesday you can offer me the hospitality of the residents' suite if I need it,' he said, plunging her into gloom once more. Then he added casually, 'Actually, I've got tickets for *Les Misérables* on Thursday. Care to come?'

Didn't' she just! 'That *would* be nice, Rory. But how come you've not already…?'

He was quick to take her meaning. 'Asked somebody? Because I like to keep my options open.'

'I see—I thought somebody must have stood you up.'

'Nobody ever stands me up,' he told her firmly, 'so don't you go getting any ideas about being the first!'

'Don't worry—I want to see that show too much to do that.'

'Charmed, I'm sure,' said Rory, unlocking the 'private' gate again.

'I could get the bus,' offered Sarah half-heatedly.

'It'd serve you right if I let you,' he said, 'but if I did, you might renege on Thursday—and then I'd have to advertise.'

'I couldn't let you do that when I'm putty in your hands,' she claimed unguardedly—and was immediately aghast. Supposing he believed that?

Rory let out a derisive hoot. 'That'll be the day!

Moulding you would be like trying to mould con-
crete. Get in, then—unless you're intending to close
the gate after I've driven out.'

'After an insult like that? Not likely, m'lad!' It
was all right. She'd done no damage with that careless admission. Keep it up, Sarah. Be jokey, light,
teasing—anything but serious. You don't want to
frighten him off.

She had him in stitches all the way back to the
hospital, but it wasn't easy. Still, if this old pals act
was all that he wanted of her, she'd do her best to
supply it. Half a loaf...

On the doorstep of the residence he kissed her—
on the cheek, as a brother would have. 'I'm really
looking forward to Thursday,' he said, giving her
bottom a friendly pat before saying goodnight.

Waiting for Thursday wasn't made any easier by
having Peter Blair ask Sarah on Wednesday if she'd
met Rory's girlfriend.

'Which one?' she asked when her heart had
stopped bounding about. 'Rumour has it he's got
several on the go.'

'Tall, red-haired, thin—and kind of haughty.'

'That sounds like Moira Stirling. She was also in
our year.'

'I wouldn't have thought she was Rory's type,'
Peter said thoughtfully.

'In my experience, any female under forty is Rory
Drummond's type,' said Sarah, most unfairly, as she
knew.

'Well, you should know—with you two being so
close,' said Peter. 'Anyway, I told Nan I'd ask you
after we saw them the other night at the Odeon,

though not to speak to. Nan wondered if we ought to ask him to bring her to our party, that's all.'

It might be all to Peter, but it was a lot more than that to Sarah. 'Next time you're just as likely to see him with a cute little blonde,' she said in what she hoped was a careless way. 'If I were you, Pete, I think I'd invite Rory and friend—or even friends, if you're short of girls. Forgive me, but I have to dash now. There's loads to do and I'm on standby tonight.'

Wednesday night was hectic, with the medical unit going like a fair. I wouldn't want to be here during the flu season, thought Sarah the fourth time she was woken up. I hope I don't yawn all through the show tomorrow—or do I mean tonight? That'll not improve my chances with Rory.

What chances? She must be going out of her mind.

She wore the red sheath again—the one she'd bought for Carrie's and Robin's engagement party— only to discover that hardly anybody dressed up for the theatre any more in Glasgow. She shrugged. She'd just have to keep her jacket on then.

Rory had also dressed down in chinos, a colourful shirt and a denim jacket. He took it off before the show began and advised Sarah to do the same. 'I'll put it under the seat with mine,' he added.

'Thanks, but I'm fine like this,' answered Sarah, opening her programme.

It was, however, a warm night and the theatre was over-heated so she was glad to peel off her jacket in the first interval.

'What a sight for sore eyes in this sea of tasteless

T-shirts,' said Rory, eyeing the expanse of smooth golden skin now revealed. 'I'll be really sorry when that gorgeous tan of yours fades.'

'I could always fake it with something out of a bottle.'

'It wouldn't be the same.'

'Then I'll just have to go back to the Med for a top-up.'

'Don't you dare leave Glasgow for the foreseeable future,' ordered Rory at his most masterful. Sarah felt quite excited. 'By the way, I got you some chocolates, though they'll likely have gone all sticky in this heat.'

'Hand them over anyway,' demanded Sarah, quite thrilled, and hoping it didn't show. 'D'you know, I've hardly eaten a thing all day? I'm starving.' She opened the box and chose the biggest one. 'And as for leaving Glasgow, I've got to. Quite soon. Unless, of course, it's off,' she mumbled with her mouth deliciously full.

'Unless what's off?' demanded Rory. 'What are you going on about now?'

She parked the chocolate in her cheek to say, 'Have you forgotten asking me to climb Ben Venue with you, then? I can't say I'm very flattered.'

'Oh, that. Of course I've not forgotten—so don't you either! I thought you were talking about another job. Which reminds me, have you rung the Dean?'

'No—not yet. There's never any time for such things during working hours.'

'Then write to him,' he urged as the lights dimmed for the next act. 'Anyway, a letter is probably best,' he whispered in her ear. His warm breath wafted deliciously down her neck. Heaven help me,

I don't even need to feel his touch, she realised as she strove to concentrate on the stage.

By the second interval the auditorium was so hot that they had to escape out to the aptly named crush bar. With so many doing the same, it was impossible to get a drink, but they ran into Tom Patterson and his wife who willingly shared their ice creams.

Explaining why Sarah was still in Glasgow and then being invited to dinner 'some time soon' took up all the time available before the slow shuffle back to their seats.

'Good, isn't it?' Rory asked obscurely as the lights were dimmed. He could have meant the show, seeing the Pattersons or just being there together.

'Marvellous,' she whispered back, inhaling his clean, masculine smell. She tried hard to concentrate on the show, which would have had her whole attention had she been with anybody else. Tonight, though, she was only aware of the man at her side.

When they emerged from the theatre into the cool, starlit night, Rory towed Sarah across the street, instead of heading for his private parking lot.

'Where are we going?' she asked.

'Would you not welcome a plate of something tasty, then?' he asked.

'Absolutely, mate, if that's also on the agenda.' I'm handling this really well, decided Sarah, even going on to admit how much she was enjoying herself.

'That's quite something, coming from you,' Rory told her. 'And I'm very glad—because I am, too.'

Sarah looked at him hopefully, but he was talking to a waiter who despaired of finding them a seat.

'But I've booked,' said Rory firmly. 'I'd be sorry if somebody has fouled up.'

'Ah, *signore*, that is different.' He led them to a small room off the main restaurant.

'Now there's thoughtful,' trilled Sarah in a mock-Welsh accent.

'Why do you sound so surprised? I am thought-ful,' declared Rory. 'I thought you knew that.'

'And so modest, too—I never realised *that*.'

They were off again, teasing and laughing but never serious, and all the time Sarah was wondering how long she could keep this up. Yet what was the alternative?

'You're off this coming weekend are you not, Sarah?' asked Rory as he handed her out of the car at the door of the residence. She couldn't remember him ever being that gallant before.

'Yes, I am—and you're on, you poor old thing.'

'No,' he said. 'I've managed to engineer a swop. So if you're still free on Saturday...'

She'd more or less arranged to go and see her brother and sister-in-law, but she said, 'As it happens, I am.'

'Would eight-thirty be too early for you?' He didn't need to say what for.

'I shall set my alarm for seven,' she said, now positively glowing with anticipation. Fortunately it didn't show in the dark.

'Good old Sarah,' said Rory, but his tone wasn't quite as playful as usual. 'Goodnight, then—and thanks for your company this evening. It was...really nice.' He put up a hand and brushed her cheek almost shyly with his fingertips. Then he got into his car and drove quickly away.

*   *   *

Next morning, Bill Ferguson phoned to ask Sarah to change duties with him again—and this time he wanted the whole weekend.

'I'm very sorry, but I'm afraid that's quite out of the question,' she replied firmly. 'My weekend is already planned and I'm not letting my friends down.'

'How about half of it, then?' he wheedled. 'Surely you can't have the whole lot spoken for?'

'I can if I'm going away—which I am. To the Trossachs.'

'But there's nobody else I can ask.'

'I'm sorry, Bill,' she repeated, 'but it's just not reasonable to expect me to change at the last minute like this.'

'My girlfriend will kill me!'

'Then she can't love you very much,' Sarah retorted. 'Right now, though, I'm too busy to argue the point.' She put the phone down. 'Honestly! Some people,' she said to Jack.

'You told him,' he said. 'Let's hope you never need a favour from him.'

'I won't,' said Sarah. 'I organise my life better. How's Charlie's leg today?'

'Much the same, which is the best we can hope for, I guess. But I'm rather worried about that old chap who came in last Thursday. He's spiking a bit of a temperature.'

'Let's make him our first call, then,' said Sarah, jumping up from the desk.

Sarah didn't see Rory to speak to all day—but she did catch a glimpse of him dashing out to his car just before five o'clock. Lucky for some, she thought and felt mean immediately afterwards. He could easily be hurrying to a domiciliary visit.

It would be at least an hour before she went off duty herself. Bill wouldn't be getting the chance to say she'd left anything undone, leaving it all to him for the weekend.

During the evening Carrie rang for a chat while Sarah was washing her hair. She wrapped a towel round her head and sat down on the bed, waiting to be entertained. She enjoyed Carrie's chats which were always full of gossip without the least trace of malice.

Today, after work, Carrie had run into Moira in Safeways and Moira had been in a furious mood. 'She's found out that Rory is still seeing that blonde nurse from the City Hospital,' she revealed.

'Moira never did like competition,' returned Sarah, in what she hoped was a nice, detached, gossipy way.

'You're absolutely right there but, as I said to her, he's got to go carefully, remembering that Dulcie is the prof's daughter and not to be slighted.

'Apparently, she'd thought—Moira, that is—that Rory would be taking her to *Les Misérables*, but he said he couldn't, yet she knew for certain that he'd got tickets for one night this week. That was bad enough, but when she heard about his big do at the City tonight—no, not actually at the hospital, but to do with it—she reckoned that standing her up for Dulcie two nights in one week was a bit thick.' Carrie giggled. 'I told her that she should have had a useful professor for a father instead of a banker. Was that not beastly of me? Anyway, she stormed off in such a tizzy that she knocked over a great stack of baked beans with her trolley!'

'Oh, Carrie!' wailed Sarah miserably, before she could stop herself.

Of course, Carrie thought that Sarah was shocked. 'I know—I'm a real cat. Anyway, how's life with you, Sarah?'

'Mustn't grumble. I'm enjoying my job and that's the main thing!'

'Naturally I'm glad about that, but you really must get out more, dear. Robin thinks so, too. Is there any chance of us seeing you this weekend? How about Sunday? Yes, come and have supper with us on Sunday. That's really why I rang—only I knew you'd be interested to hear about my little brush with Moira.'

Not to mention Rory and that Dulcie! 'Thanks, Carrie, dear, I'd love to come on Sunday, if you're sure it's no trouble.'

Carrie laughed at the very idea, told Sarah not to be a goose and any time after seven would be fine, but now she really must prepare something nice and light for Robin. 'He's on this weekend, poor darling, and he'll be absolutely whacked when he does get home.'

Sarah finished drying her hair. Naturally, it was depressing to hear all about Rory and his women, but it did help her to keep a sense of proportion. Once or twice the previous night she'd caught herself wondering if he was at last beginning to see her as special. How could she have been so naïve?

CHAPTER SIX

AFTER years abroad, Sarah was short of clothes suitable for a day on the hills in Scotland, so some thickish cotton shorts, a shirt and a sweater—just in case—would have to do. Luckily, she'd unearthed her old hiking boots and some thick socks from the trunk her brother had been keeping for her.

She'd thought she was on time, but when she went downstairs Rory was already there. 'Another five minutes and I'd have been throwing stones up at your window,' he greeted her.

'That would certainly have set the tongues wagging,' said Sarah. And he'd not want that.

'Think so?' He stole a quick sideways glance as she took her seat beside him. 'No more than you telling everybody we were going away together for the weekend.'

'I never said anything of the sort!' she denied vigorously. 'Unless…' she'd suddenly remembered what she'd said to Bill. 'When the SHO on Geriatrics asked me to swop weekends, I said I couldn't possibly as I was going to the Trossachs. I did not say who with—or for how long.'

Rory chuckled wickedly. 'That was quite enough to start a fire when Pete knows I'm heading that way—and with whom.'

'And they try to tell us it's only women who gossip! So how was your evening?' she shot at him.

'Which one?' he asked after a minute.

'Last night's gala or whatever.'

'Oh, that evening. It was all right—quite pleasant, actually. The Friends of the City Hospital hold a fund-raising do every year about this time and it's more than one's life is worth not to turn up.'

'But you're not at the City now.'

'I was when I got roped in for it—and I couldn't let them down, could I? It would've upset the numbers at dinner. It's quite a formal affair.'

For 'them' read 'Dulcie', yet his explanation was very convincing on the face of it. Sarah decided to reserve judgement. 'Dinner—and then dancing, I suppose. I love dancing…'

'I remember. Yes, it was a dinner dance.'

'Then you should have postponed today's climb—or started later. You must be exhausted.'

'Sarah, I am twenty-nine—not ninety-two! I am not exhausted and I didn't want to cancel,' he added firmly.

'It would certainly have been a shame to miss such a lovely day,' returned Sarah, sounding more serene than she felt.

'Very true—so let's not spoil it by bickering.'

She couldn't think how to reply to such a sensible remark, so she pretended to be engrossed in the scenery.

'Anything wrong, Sary, lass?' asked Rory after a mile or two.

She realised with a jolt that that was the first time he'd called her Sary since she'd told him she was going away with Steve. 'I… Just thinking that I've not written to the Dean yet.' It was the first excuse to come into her head. 'I suppose you think that's silly.'

'Not silly exactly, but I wouldn't leave it much longer. I hear that he's off to the States quite soon for several weeks.'

'Then I'll write tomorrow—definitely. I can't afford to be unemployed.'

'I dare say your old mates would see to it that you didn't starve,' he said humorously as they topped the rise on the Duke's pass and a panorama of Lochs Achray and Venachar lay below them. 'Beat that for a view,' he challenged.

'Who could? Oh, Rory! I did miss all this while…' Now, of course, he would say something smart along the lines of, I told you so!

He didn't. Instead, he reached across and squeezed her knee. 'Look forward—not back, you silly old thing,' he said quietly. And then he added more matter-of-factly, 'I'll bet you forgot to bring any lunch.'

Sarah bit her lip. 'I've got apples and some chocolate…'

'And I've brought sandwiches and coffee. We'll survive.'

'Let's hope so,' she responded mechanically. Her knee was still tingling from his touch.

The car park at the foot of the mountain was already full, but Rory managed to squeeze his car into a tiny woodland clearing beside it. Then they set off to tackle the mountain by the steepest route. That meant that little was said beyond the necessary until they reached the top.

The view was spectacular. Below lay wooded hills and sparkling lochs. To the south-west they could see the misty hills of Arran, while the Grampians stood stark and rugged in the opposite

direction. Despite the sun, it was cool up here and
Rory decided they should eat their lunch in the shel-
ter of an overhang of rock some thirty feet below
the summit. Besides, it was crowded at the top on
such a lovely day.

They still weren't talking much; there seemed no
need. Sarah took off her sweater and lay basking in
the sun—and the sheer luxury of just being there
with the man she loved. She glanced at him covertly
through half-closed eyes. Thick hair which was
never quite tidy, straight brows, firm jaw, strong
muscular limbs—and she thought, Oh, Rory, Rory.
Has fate thrown us together again for nothing?

Rory had been watching Sarah when he was sure
she wasn't looking, but when he spoke it was only
to say, 'I don't like that bank of cloud away to the
south-west. With the wind from that direction, it
could easily catch us before we reach the bottom.'

Sarah sat up, looking disappointed. 'Must we really go now, Rory? Even if we go down the easy
way?' She wanted to prolong this idyll. Who knew
if there'd ever be another?

'I was intending to do that anyway,' he said. 'Do
you want another coffee before we go?'

'No, thanks.'

He uncapped the flask and poured the remainder
onto the ground. 'No sense in carrying more than
we have to,' he said.

So soon afterwards, they set off back down the
mountain. Being experienced hill-walkers, they leapt
easily from outcrop to outcrop. They were making
very good time, but the mist caught them before
they were halfway down, thick, swirling and cold.

Sarah stopped to put on her sweater and wished she was wearing trousers rather than shorts.

'Don't move until I get our bearings,' Rory ordered. 'There must be no straying from the path from here on down. About five feet to your left, carefully now...'

He was right, of course, and when they'd located the main track, he took a rope from his rucksack and tied it to Sarah's belt. 'You're out of practice, flower,' he said when she protested. 'And I don't trust you not to get lost.'

'Just so long as you keep hold of the other end...'

'Would I ever let you down?' he asked.

'Certainly not halfway up a mountain.' She was sure of that.

They felt their way cautiously step by step down the path for almost an hour until they came to the only really steep bit on this route. That was when they heard voices and somebody groaning.

'Somebody's not been too lucky,' said Rory, seconds before their way was barred by a middle-aged man most inadequately clothed in floral shorts, a thin T-shirt and canvas sneakers. 'I don't suppose there's any chance you're a doctor?' he asked.

'Why?' asked Rory. 'Is somebody hurt?'

They heard another groan. 'That's the wife,' said the man. 'She's sprained her ankle or summat. Thanks to this bloody fog.'

'Not to mention her footwear,' murmured Rory, having located the injured woman and noted her flimsy sandals.

'It says easy for this walk in the guide book,' continued the man crossly. 'They should 'ave said about the fog.'

'Perhaps it wasn't foggy the day the book was written,' Rory said dryly as he rummaged in his rucksack for bandages.

'Is it bad, Doctor?' asked the woman, who knew experienced hands when she felt them.

'Too bad for you to walk on it at any rate,' Rory said firmly. 'I'll fix you up with a firm support and give you something for the pain, but it's best if you both wait here until we can get a stretcher party to you.'

'What about the bus?' objected the man. 'We're on a tour, like. You got a mobile?'

'If I had, it'd not be much use up here,' said Rory patiently as he continued bandaging.

'That looks grand,' the man deigned to say when Rory had finished. 'Come on, ole gel. You can manage if you lean on me.'

'She most certainly cannot,' said Rory in a tone that forbade argument. 'Your wife has almost certainly fractured her tibia—the main leg bone—just above the ankle.'

'You an' me'll 'ave to carry 'er, then, squire.'

'I think not. The path is far too treacherous in this mist.' He didn't point out that, besides being physically unfit, the man was no better shod than his unfortunate wife. 'My friend and I will fetch help, but you must stay put.' He handed them a packet. 'Here, wrap yourselves in this—you'll need it.'

'Silver bloody paper,' said the man disgustedly.

'No, an anti-hypothermia blanket,' Rory corrected curtly.

Sarah plucked at his sleeve. 'Rory, do you think I ought to stay with them?' she whispered. 'They really have no idea of the danger they're in.'

He'd been thinking along the same lines, but he didn't want to leave her.

'You stay—you're the doctor—and let *her* go,' said the woman.

'No. I will go and Dr Sinclair will stay with you,' Rory decided unwillingly, realising that the daft pair couldn't be left by themselves.

'D'you hear that, gel? Two bleedin' doctors! This is your lucky day,' said her husband, who was clearly anything but Mensa material.

Rory folded Sarah into his cagoule. 'For God's sake, be careful,' she begged as he melted into the mist.

It seemed an age before she heard the voices of the rescue party, but when she looked at her watch she realised it was less than two hours since Rory had left them. Despite her warning, he must have gone down the hill like a rocket.

'Are you all right, Sarah?' They were his first words as he loomed out of the mist.

'Everything's fine…more or less,' she said in an undertone. The two tourists had kept up an incessant grumbling all the time, and she had got tired of spelling out the difficulties.

'And I had the most amazing bit of luck, finding these two chaps in the car park. That's why I'm back so soon.'

'Call this soon?' asked the man, but everybody ignored him. The two countryside rangers were too busy transferring the casualty carefully onto a stretcher and Sarah was telling Rory that she'd had to give Mrs Finch another dose of DF 118. She lowered her voice still further. 'I was sorely tempted to give the rest of it to him, just to shut him up, but I resisted the temptation. It would have been to difficult getting him down the track.'

Rory chuckled. 'Very clear-headed of you, but, then, you always were—medically speaking.'

It was soon decided that Rory would head the procession, followed by Mr Finch, then by the rangers with the stretcher and finally Sarah. 'And, for God's sake, be careful, Sary,' begged Rory. 'The next hundred feet is the worst on this route.'

Mr Finch objected. 'I reckon the old woman should go before me—I mean, what if they drop her? I'd get it in the neck.'

'You'll do as you're told!' snapped his wife, whose patience had worn thin. 'And you'll get it in the neck all right if you don't give over!' She was surprisingly alert for one so recently sedated. Her foot was obviously very painful, so Rory's diagnosis had been spot on.

He had also been right about the state of the track. It took two hours to reach the car park and the mist stayed with them all the way.

The rangers lifted Mrs Finch carefully into their Land Rover and bundled her husband in beside her.

'How about that?' asked Rory. 'They make a right mess of our day off and they go without a word of thanks.'

'That's too often the way, as we should know,' said the senior ranger. 'Now what about you two, Doc? Can we drop you anywhere?'

'That's very decent of you, but we've got our own transport.'

'Just so long as you've not missed your bus with all the delay…'

Rory said again how glad he'd been to see the

two men there earlier, then he and Sarah watched as the Land Rover eased onto the road then turned right towards Stirling and the nearest hospital. Then they strolled down to the other end of the car park and the little clearing where they had left his car. Then they halted abruptly and stared in utter disbelief. Rory's car had disappeared.

'This can't be the right place,' he said after several seconds of stunned silence. 'We must have missed it in the fog. You must be whacked, Sary, so you stay here while I look around.'

Not as whacked as you, my darling, after your double journey up and down that hill, she thought, but she did as she'd been told and stayed put.

He wasn't away long. 'I've been right to the bend in the road and there's no other place big enough to hold a car,' he reported heavily. 'This has to be where we left it. Some bastard's nicked it!'

'Are there any cars still in the car park?' Sarah asked practically.

'No—I looked. We'll just have to make for Aberfoyle and hope that somebody comes by and gives us a lift.' He laughed bitterly. 'You must be wishing you'd never come out with me today.'

'Don't be silly,' she said indignantly, linking her arm through his. 'It was a wonderful day—if you leave out those Finches—and who'd have thought the car would be stolen out in the country? If it had been in the city, now...'

'It wasn't in the car park, though.'

'You think that would have made a difference? Well, I don't! What did was the fog—and you can't blame yourself for that, so don't try!'

'Oh, Sarah!' He put his arms right round her and

hugged her hard. 'If there's anybody in the whole world I'd choose to share a tight spot with, it's you!'

'You're fairly reliable yourself,' she said in a muffled voice. She was half-suffocated against his chest, but so happy.

'You can't imagine how good it feels to have you back,' he admitted as he let go of her, while keeping hold of her hand. 'Nobody else has ever quite filled the place you had in my life.'

It would have been easier to have made the right reply if she'd known exactly what he'd meant by that. Before Rory could say anything, they heard the sound of an engine. Rory let go of her and rushed to the roadside, but too late to stop a battered van. 'Going the wrong way in any case,' he said philosophically. 'Got all your gear, hen? Right. Best foot forward. Surely we'll get to Aberfoyle before the last bus goes.'

They hadn't gone more than fifty yards before they came upon a rusty old banger with its nearside wheels in the ditch.

'It must have run off the road in the fog,' diagnosed Rory, giving it a shove.

'I know you're strong,' said Sarah, 'but you're not strong enough to get it back on the road, so forget it.'

He laughed with genuine amusement. 'I wasn't going to try a Hercules—just wondering if it belongs to the thieves.' He found a scrap of paper in his pocket and made a note of the number.

'More than likely,' agreed Sarah. 'I wonder where they're headed?'

'Straight to gaol, I hope, if they make a habit of it. Listen, did you hear an engine?'

They stood with bated breath for several seconds, but the sound died away. 'Not even on this road,' said Rory with a sigh.

They trudged on, getting wetter and wetter as the mist turned to drizzle and then to rain. They reached Aberfoyle in time to see the tail-light of the last bus for Glasgow disappear in gloom. By then they were very cold, very wet and very hungry.

Rory took Sarah's hand and towed her towards the nearest hotel. 'I've been here before,' he said. 'It's not the Ritz, but it's clean, warm and comfortable.' Having settled her beside a blazing fire in the lounge with a brandy and a menu, he went to phone the local police station. He was gone some time.

'What did they say?' Sarah asked eagerly when he returned.

Rory dropped wearily down on the bench beside her. 'An answering machine told me to leave a message and a telephone number, or to contact Stirling if it was an emergency.'

'So what did you say?'

'By emergency, it seems they mean murder, arson or civil war—not anything as trivial as a stolen car and two stranded hikers. So I left a message as instructed and added a few colourful thoughts on the so-called progress which has led to the disappearance of the local bobby. But not until I'd replaced the phone, you'll be glad to hear.'

'I think that was wonderfully restrained of you,' said Sarah admiringly. 'I'd have phoned HQ and given them an earful.'

Rory grinned. 'I don't doubt that. You always did have a sizeable paddy. You should have had red

hair—not such a wonderful cloud of black silk...'
He reached out and curled a strand round his finger.

That gesture would have had Sarah over the moon
if only he hadn't mentioned red hair, which brought
Moira to mind. 'Get along with you,' she said, jerking free. 'I've ordered us soup and a main course. I
hope steak pie was a good guess for you.'

'Just what I'd have chosen.' He looked at her
questioningly. 'I don't suppose you asked about accommodation?'

'No, I didn't.'

'Well, we're definitely going to need somewhere
to lay our heads tonight. After the police, I phoned
my insurance company, and they can't get a courtesy car to me before tomorrow—in Glasgow.'

'Could we hire a car in the village? I've got no
clothes or anything.'

'Do you suppose I have?' he asked. 'Somehow I
never think of pyjamas and a toothbrush as musts
for a walk.'

Sarah bit her lip, feeling rather silly, but the arrival of soup provided a diversion. It was brought
by the proprietor, whom Rory obviously knew. 'Yes,
Doc, we can fix you up, as it happens,' he said,
when asked. 'A couple on the coach tour got into
trouble out walking this afternoon and landed up in
Stirling Royal infirmary, so you can have their
room.' Room—not rooms! 'Bit of luck for you, eh?
Otherwise, we'd be full.'

Sarah opened her mouth and shut it again in obe-
dience to Rory's warning look. 'Like it or not, half
a loaf is always better than no bread,' he told her
when the man had gone.

Just what she was always telling herself where he was concerned. 'Yes, I know,' she answered quietly.

Rory was very surprised at such meekness but decided not to question it. 'Good soup,' he said, tucking in. And added with the ghost of a smile, 'Being obliged to the Finches for a night's lodging is quite a coincidence.'

'The very least they could do, some would say— but why do you suppose they're both in hospital?'

'I doubt if they are. He must have had a belated attack of husbandly concern and decided to stay to provide support.'

'Think so? My guess is that he missed the last bus back to Aberfoyle.'

'You're a cynic, Sarah.'

He'd told her that more than once and she didn't like it. 'Do you mind? I prefer to see myself as a realist. And, heavens, Rory, I've just remembered I've only got about ten pounds on me. How are you fixed?'

'Credit card,' he said. 'I never go out without it.'

'Nor do I normally, but not on a country walk. Supposing I lost it?'

'It'd be safe enough if you did what I do and stuck it inside your sock.' He grinned wryly. 'With me, it's only cars that get stolen.'

'I don't think I could be so sanguine if it'd happened to me. You're a very good person to be in a tight spot with,' Sarah said impulsively, which was more or less what Rory had said to her when they'd realised the car had gone. Only he'd said it with his arms around her...

'You're blushing,' said Rory, watching her colour rising.

'No, I'm not—it's the heat of the fire,' she insisted, pulling her sweater off over her head and stuffing it into her haversack.

By then Rory's eyes had homed in on a spot well below the level of her chin. 'You'd better do up a few buttons unless you want to cause a riot,' he said.

Sarah glanced down and saw that her shirt was undone almost to the waist. She began to button up. 'Sorry about that. Still, it's not as though you were…almost any other man.'

'Meaning?'

'You've never thought of me in *that* way, have you?'

'Did you ever want me to?' he asked as she did up the last button.

Why the hell couldn't he have given her a straight answer? Sarah went for safety. 'I'm just an old-fashioned girl who's never seen the point in mooning over a man who obviously didn't fancy me,' she claimed as her empty soup bowl was whipped away and replaced by a mound of lamb cutlets and vegetables. 'I expect a man to—to pursue me if he's interested.'

'And look where that got you,' said Rory. 'Perhaps you should modernise. Be a bit more forthcoming. There's no shame in letting a man know if you like him. Don't you realise that a man's got to be pretty conceited to try breaking down a stone wall?'

He was looking quite het up, but he was thinking like a brother again. Had to be, because when was Rory Drummond ever backward in coming forward? We've known each other too long and too well as friends ever to be anything more, surmised Sarah with a sinking heart. Half a loaf… 'Eat your dinner,' she said like a chum. 'It must be getting cold.'

Rory regarded her steadily for perhaps ten seconds, before letting out his breath on a long sigh. Then he picked up his knife and fork and did what he'd been told.

After supper they had coffee and then a drink at the bar with some friendly locals, so it was well after midnight when they followed the proprietor up to the room that should have been the Finches. 'What's all this?' asked Rory, on seeing the night gear laid out on the beds.

'Courtesy of me and the wife,' said the proprietor. 'We reckoned it was the least we could do. Breakfast at eight—if that's OK with you?'

They thanked him and he went, after wishing them pleasant dreams.

Sarah picked up the huge, long-sleeved, high-necked winceyette nightgown from the nearest bed. It would have gone round her at least twice and she collapsed, giggling. When she could speak, she said, 'I'd be safe in this from even the most determined sex maniac.'

'And quite safe from your old pal—in case you were wondering,' said Rory woodenly.

Her laughter ceased on the instant. 'I know that,' she said quietly. 'I never for a moment supposed otherwise. Would you like the bathroom first?'

'Be my guest,' he said in the same lifeless voice.

When Sarah came back, holding up handfuls of nightie so as not to trip over it, Rory was gazing moodily out of the window. He hadn't removed so much as a sweater. 'The sky is quite clear now,' he announced, without turning round.

'I don't care what it looks like—I'm not going anywhere till morning,' declared Sarah, leaping into bed and pulling the duvet up to her chin.

Rory did turn round then. 'The last time I saw you in bed was when you were hospitalised with glandular fever,' he said slowly.

'In our third year, that was—and, as far as I remember, that was the *only* time you've ever seen me in bed.' She paused. 'Seeing you likewise will be a first for me.' Just saying that had provoked a deplorable frisson. Oh, God! How would she manage not to fling herself at him? But she must, or lose him as a friend…

'I hope it'll not be a dreadful disappointment,' Rory said roughly, snatching up the pyjamas provided and disappearing into the bathroom.

When he reopened the door, it was only by the merest crack. He called out, 'Switch off the light, Sarah, there's a pal.'

'Not on your life,' she said.

'All right—but if you laugh, I swear I'll kill you,' he warned, sidling into the room.

She fell about laughing immediately. The pyjama jacket didn't come within inches of fastening and the trousers reached no further than mid-calf. When she'd recovered, she stripped off the nightgown, keeping the duvet for covering, and tossed it to him. 'Swop,' she commanded. 'It's the sensible thing.'

He raised his eyebrows. 'I don't really think it's my colour, do you? I'll just have to go bare!'

Sarah looked the other way to hide her blushes. She gave a smothered gulp, and then said, 'Just the jacket will do for me.' She wriggled under the duvet to put it on quickly, before lying down again.

Rory turned out the light, before getting into bed. After a long moment he said tentatively, 'Sarah?'

'Yes, Rory?'

'I…wish with all my heart that this day could have ended…differently.'

'I'm sure you do,' she said sadly.

'You understand what I'm saying?' She could almost hear him straining for her reply, so she'd better get it right.

'Of course I do! Right place, wrong girl. Unless, of course, it's only the car that's bugging you?'

'You got some of it right,' he said after another long pause. 'Goodnight, then.'

Sarah lay awake for hours, eventually falling into such a heavy sleep that Rory had to wake her. Rousing, opening her eyes and seeing him bending over her, it was like an extension of her dream. 'Rory, darling,' she murmured drowsily, reaching up for him.

She wasn't fully awake until she was in his arms and she was panic-stricken when she realised how she must have given herself away. She stiffened and tried to break free. 'So sorry—can't think what came over me. Thought you were…at least three other people—'

'Stop it, Sarah!'

His kiss was more effective than any words and it left her weak and longing for more. 'Oh, Rory…'

'Oh, Sarah,' he mimicked, rocking her gently in his arms with his cheek against hers.

She couldn't—daren't—believe that he wasn't just humouring her. If she wasn't still asleep… 'You don't have to pretend—I was half asleep. Dreaming. I never meant— Sorry…'

He held her away from him and looked at her sternly. 'What does it take to get through to you?' he demanded. 'This thing is mutual, you enchanting idiot.'

'You…actually *like* me…?' she whispered, beginning to believe at last.

'If that's the way you want to put it.'

'Oh, Rory,' she murmured blissfully when he'd kissed her again. She wound her arms round his neck just as there came a thunderous knocking at the door. 'My God, what was that?' she breathed.

'The chambermaid. That's why I had to come up and wake you. She's done all the other rooms and is desperate to get finished.'

'What time is it, then?'

'Just gone half past nine.'

'Is that all?'

'Get up—please, love, before I lose my head and jump on you,' he begged.

'I'd like that,' said Sarah as the irate maid thrust her passkey in the lock.

'Why could you not have told me that last night?' He sighed, yanking off the duvet and calling out, 'Ten minutes. She's nearly ready.'

Except on duty, Sarah had never dressed so fast in her life. 'I haven't washed,' she protested.

'You had a bath last night,' he reminded her, stuffing her into her sweater just as they were nearly knocked flying by the woman whose patience was exhausted. She was six feet tall and built accordingly.

'No wonder you were in such a hurry to get me up—she's terrifying,' breathed Sarah when they were out on the landing, bag and baggage.

'I think the proprietor agrees with you,' said Rory. 'She's his wife—which explains the nightgown.'

'I'm surprised he dared to lend it out,' returned Sarah as they rounded the last bend in the stairs. 'Now what do we do?'

'I suggest we head back to Glasgow on the next bus. There'll be no hill-walking the day.'

Sarah had already noted the leaden skies and relentless rain. 'I couldn't agree more, though I'd not say no to something to eat first.'

'And you shall have something, my treasure—there's a decent wee café in the main street where we can keep an eye on the bus terminus at the same time.'

'No news of the car, I suppose,' said Sarah when they were in the café and out of the rain.

'Not a word, but I've left another message on that answering machine—for all the good that'll do.'

'Whatever happens, you've done all you can—it's up to the police now. Good heavens!' she exclaimed on seeing the size of the breakfast he'd ordered for her. 'What time is the bus?'

'Not till half ten, and if you can't get through that lot by then, I'll help you.'

He was finishing the last sausage when the bus came in and they had to dash through the rain to join the queue. Many other hill-walkers had given up in disgust at the weather, and the bus was packed. They were nearly back to Glasgow before they were able to sit together. Then Rory said, 'Do you realise that we'll be passing the Allanbank very soon?'

'Yes—why? Do you want to get rid of me?'

'A silly question like that deserves a silly answer, but I was only going to suggest that you should pop in for a few things to take you through until tomorrow.'

'Tomorrow,' she echoed, giving him a bright glance.

'You're off duty till then—remember? And you'll love my new flat,' he added on a pulse-raising murmur.

'Practical as well as dishy,' purred Sarah. 'I like that in a man.'

'And you're so dishy I could eat you,' Rory whispered as the bus screeched to a halt at the hospital gates.

Rory decided that as he was there anyway, he might as well nip up to Orthopaedics and check on things there while Sarah packed a bag. 'I'll see you at the front entrance in ten minutes,' he said, kissing her full on the mouth and causing a porter to steer his trolley into a wall.

Humming a happy tune, Sarah sped up to her room. Before she'd quite finished packing, the phone rang. Her first reaction was to ignore it as she was off duty, but then she thought it could be Rory.

'Ah, Sarah—splendid. You were seen coming in,' said the most senior of the medical registrars, of whom all the juniors were in awe.

'Only to pick up something, Dr Cairns. I'm off duty this weekend.'

'Not any more, you're not. Dr Ferguson has reported sick.'

'No!' snarled Sarah. 'I won't. It's not fair. If I'd not come in you'd not have known where—'

'But you did, Sarah, and you're needed. Report to me in the acute respiratory unit in ten minutes and I'll give you a briefing.'

'And if I refuse?' But Sarah knew she had no choice.

'I hope you'll not be so foolish,' said the dragon in arctic tones. 'That wouldn't look too good on your CV, would it?'

'All right, then—ten minutes,' said Sarah, but she meant to see Rory first and explain.

She was surprised and disappointed at his reaction when she told him what had happened, but then he revealed that he'd heard a whisper of the crisis on his own unit. 'Yes, darling, it's damnable,' he said soothingly, 'but unfortunately it's all part of the job.'

'Don't you *mind*?' she asked, not liking such restraint on his part.

'Of course I mind, but it's no used getting steamed up over something we can't help.' His face darkened. 'If I could just get my hands on those thieves! But for them, this would never have happened.'

Because the quickest route to his part of the city from the Trossachs was nowhere near the hospital. But then, neither would they have stayed away overnight—with such wonderful results.

Sarah gave him a quick kiss and told him not to forget her. 'Have a nice day,' she called back jauntily as she hurried to her briefing.

CHAPTER SEVEN

'IT IS now seventeen minutes since I told you to report to me in ten, Doctor,' said Dr Maureen Cairns, baring her teeth in a spiteful smile across the desk.

Doesn't believe in a body having a private life, thought Sarah mutinously. No wonder she and Miss Coull are such pals. 'I had to explain to my boyfriend why my off-duty has been cancelled,' she answered quietly but firmly.

The smile disappeared. 'You were asked to step into the breach and you agreed,' Sarah was told. 'Now, then. There are two seriously ill patients on this unit who require half-hourly assessment, intravenous drug therapy and blood gases.'

'Anything else?' asked Sarah grimly.

'You will take all routine calls to medical cases—and refer anything you can't handle to me.'

'Well, thank you for your trust,' said Sarah. 'In my experience, patients such as the two you described are usually monitored by a registrar.'

That's telling her, she thought, taking care to get out of the office before the old tabby exploded. But how the blazes does she think I can take all the calls, as well as spending quite half my time here? One thing was sure—it would be Monday now before she'd have time to write that letter to the Dean.

She went first to the patients in respiratory failure and found them to be every bit as ill as she'd feared.

'I'll be very surprised if these two are not put on ventilators within the next twenty-four hours,' she confided to the staff nurse who was looking after them.

'It's been touch and go since they came in,' revealed the girl, 'but you know how the anaesthetists delay as long as possible because of damage to the trachea.'

'Quite right, too, except that with these two...' Sarah shrugged. 'See you in half an hour, then.'

'Don't you go killing yourself,' advised the nurse. 'If you can't make it every time, I'll just get the lovely Maureen off her great backside. The exercise will do her good,' she was winding up with relish when Sarah got a call to her own unit.

She was met in the corridor by Jack Kinnear, looking grave. 'It's dear old Charlie,' he said as he hurried her along. 'He's having a coronary—and not a small one by the look of it.'

It took time to stabilise him, so Sarah asked if somebody could please ring Acute Respiratory and explain. 'He should really be in the coronary care unit,' she was telling Jack a little later, 'but they're full already and, anyway, it might distress him. He's quite at home here.'

'Exactly,' agreed Jack, 'and you can rely on me to see he gets all the care he needs.' He took a last troubled look at the old man as they left the bedside. 'Tell me honestly, Sarah—is he going to make it?'

'I don't know,' she answered slowly. 'His spirit is wonderful, but he's an old man and this is a serious attack.'

'I hope he does pull through,' Jack said. 'Originally he came in for a week, but with all his other little problems it's stretched to two months and now the place wouldn't be the same without him.'

'Buzz me immediately if there's any change,' urged Sarah, 'otherwise I'll be back the first free minute I get.'

Jack suddenly remembered. 'I thought you were off this weekend.'

'So did I, but life is full of surprises.'

'Well, I can't say I'm sorry about this one,' Jack replied as her pager went off again.

It was a call to Geriatrics this time and another cardiac episode which proved to be a mild one. Then it was back to the two patients Dr Cairns had given into her charge, then back to Charlie. There was no let-up until well after six, when the duty consultant anaesthetist came to check on the two patients who were borderline ventilation cases. He made positive decisions for both, and once they were safely attached to ventilators Sarah was able to relax a bit.

She realised she was hungry, checked her watch and suddenly remembered she was supposed to be having supper with Carrie and Robin. A phone call took care of that and then it was time to check on Charlie again. There was no change in his condition, which was the most that could be hoped for.

As soon as she could, Sarah seized another moment to phone Rory's flat, but there was no reply. Could he be on his way here with another take-away, like last weekend? It was a nice thought, even though she'd never find time to eat it...

By morning, Sarah was absolutely whacked, and even Miss Coull noticed when she chanced to step out of her office as Sarah was passing. 'Is it usual for SHOs to be on duty two weekends in succession?' she asked.

Sarah explained about Dr Ferguson being off sick, which Miss Coull found very interesting as she had seen him going into a restaurant in Town the night before. 'In the company of a very fast-looking young woman,' she added.

Naturally Sarah was furious, but on reflection she decided she'd have been more upset if it had been Rory the UNO had seen. He hadn't phoned her the evening before, as he'd promised to, and he'd been out when she'd phoned him. Remembering that, she didn't go straight up to him when she saw him in the canteen, but waited for him to come to her.

'You look quite drained, darling,' he said, and the concern in his voice was only partly comforting.

'Well, thank you,' she said. 'To know I look a wreck is all I was needing.'

'I'm sorry,' he said tenderly. 'That was tactless of me when you've obviously had a terrible twenty-four hours. I knew you were having a bad time when that woman said you were too busy to come to the phone.'

'Which woman—when?' Sarah asked suspiciously.

'Last evening. They tracked you to the acute chest unit, and she said she'd take a message as you couldn't come to the phone.'

'What did she sound like?' asked Sarah, though she was pretty sure she could guess who it had been.

'Very fierce and very Aberdonian.'

'I knew it—Maureen Cairns! Needless to say, the old cat did not give me your message.

'So what did you do with yourself last night?' she asked when she'd finished fuming.

Rory collected the soup they'd decided on and steered Sarah towards a vacant table.

'Not what I'd expected—and hoped for—that's for sure,' he told her with a heart-stopping little grin.

'A quiet and lonely evening all by yourself, then?' she suggested hopefully.

'Exactly,' he agreed. 'I say, this soup is better than usual.'

'Too much pepper for my taste,' Sarah returned grimly. He was lying—or why hadn't he answered the phone when she'd rung?

'All alone for the whole evening,' she pressed. 'I don't suppose that happens to you very often…'

'Just what old Ali said,' he returned artlessly.

'And who exactly is old Ali?' asked Sarah, baffled.

'The chap who keeps our corner shop. He has a very decent delicatessen so I got something for supper when I went for the *Sunday Times*. ''Not often you're at a loose end on a Sunday night, Doc,'' he said. That's what I like about these corner shopkeepers. As well as stocking practically everything one could possibly want, they take an interest in their regulars.'

Sarah was less interested in Rory's retail philosophy than in finding out when and for how long he'd been out of his flat. She began her research by asking what time he'd tried to ring her.

He grinned and said he supposed she was checking up on the dragon. 'Let me see now,' he continued slowly. 'The first time was about six, but I rang again later when you didn't call me back. That would have been after I'd been to the shop. I'd had half a mind to come out and see you, but with you being so busy and not knowing how the buses run on a Sunday I gave up and waited for you to ring me—which you didn't.'

It fitted, she reckoned—or very nearly. Of all the darnedest things...

'I'm sorry,' she said warmly. She meant for not trusting him, but, naturally, Rory thought she meant for not ringing.

'Darling, it wasn't your fault,' he said. 'How could you possibly know if you hadn't been told?' He dropped his voice to a caressing whisper. 'Why not come back with me tonight for some pampering...and so on?'

'I can't, Rory, I'm on standby again,' she had to say. 'You know that SHOs always are after a weekend off.'

'That's monstrous!' he returned heatedly. 'Besides, you weren't off.'

'I was officially, and I've already tried to swop but nobody was willing—or able.'

'It's monstrous,' he repeated, but they both knew there was nothing to be done.

'I shall stay here, then, and ply you with coffee between calls,' he decided.

Sarah was very tempted, but honesty obliged her to point out, 'If tonight is anything like last night—and something tells me it will be—there'll be no time for coffee or anything else.'

He smiled at her, lifting her flagging spirits. 'Besides, you never did like mixing business with pleasure, did you? Could be that's why we never got this far before.'

The reason they'd not got very far before was because he'd never wanted them to, but he'd obviously forgotten that.

'So when are we both off together?' pursued Rory. 'You'll be off tomorrow, but I'll be on—'

'And we'll both be off on Wednesday,' Sarah put in eagerly. 'Unless, of course, you've already got a date,' she added when he didn't immediately answer.

'Nothing that can't be changed, so—' He was interrupted by Sarah's pager.

'That'll be Dr Marshall, wanting to know if I've forgotten the clinic,' she guessed. 'Give me a ring later, huh?'

'I'll certainly try,' said Rory with a rueful grin as she scuttled away.

'Are you ill, Sarah?' asked the consultant as soon as he saw her.

'No, sir—just a bit tired.' She told him as briefly as possible about having to stand in for a sick colleague for part of the weekend. 'And it was as hectic as I've ever known it,' she added.

'How unfortunate that you dropped in yesterday,' he said. 'I'll warrant that's a mistake you'll not make again. Our own unit is fairly quiet, though, so I suggest you get away sharpish and treat yourself to an early night.'

Easier said than done. 'Actually, I'm on again tonight, sir—officially.'

'Then get somebody to change with you.'

'I did try, but the notice was too short.'

'Then we can only hope that things will be better tonight. Now, then, have you had any luck, finding joint accommodation for that old couple you were so worried about last week?'

'None at all.' She sighed. 'And I'm dreading having to tell them.'

'A new long-stay geriatric unit is opening shortly at the old Larkfield Hospital, and if I'm not mistaken there are to be some rooms for couples. It's a good way out of the city but, from what you say, the Griersons' children don't visit them much now so they can hardly complain about the extra distance.'

'Oh, Dr Marshall, that's wonderful!' cried Sarah. 'I'm so pleased. They're such a dear old pair—and so devoted, it's heart-warming.'

'Steady on, Sarah—it's still only a possibility.' He smiled. 'You've got a kind heart, lassie, and that's not a bad thing in a doctor—as long as you manage to keep a sense of proportion. And now we'd better find out what's in store for us today.'

But today there was nobody with such an acute problem as the Griersons on Sarah's list and the clinic only overran by half an hour—a record. She had just finished the paperwork when the phone rang. It was Dr Cairns.

'Sarah? Glad I caught you. Just a call to let you know that Dr Ferguson will be duty medical SHO tonight.'

'I thought he was supposed to be ill!' Sarah cried impulsively.

'You'll be glad to hear that he is fully recovered so you'll not be needed tonight.' She hung up before Sarah could comment further.

It didn't take long to work out what had happened. Miss Coull had told her friend Dr Cairns what she'd seen the night before and Dr Cairns had

Taken Steps. I'd not want to be in Bill Ferguson's shoes, thought Sarah as she went to check on Charlie.

One look at Jack's face was enough. 'When?' she asked in a whisper.

'About half an hour ago—it was very sudden and peaceful.'

'Has anybody...?'

'Dr Gray was here for once, and she confirmed death,' said Jack, to Sarah's relief. She'd been very fond of the old man.

'Sudden and peaceful, you said. Just what we'd all wish for ourselves, Jack. Come along to the doctors' room. I think we could both do with a cuppa.'

It was a measure of Sarah's preoccupation with Charlie and her other patients that she'd gone off duty and was wallowing in a hot bath before she realised that now she could see Rory tonight after all. He wasn't going out—he'd said as much—so she would give him a nice surprise!

She dressed carefully in a summer skirt and jacket of biscuit-coloured linen and did her best to disguise the shadows under her eyes with make-up. Then she ordered a taxi because taking two buses, as she'd have had to, would have meant the evening would have been half over before she'd got there.

Rory's flat was in a refurbished tenement block on the fringe of the genteel district of Kelvinside. Sara rang the bell twice. Then she walked round the block before ringing it a third time, just to make sure that he really wasn't at home.

At first she felt foolish. It was her own fault for coming without warning. Then she began to feel cross with him for painting such a pathetic picture of himself alone and lonely when he'd very likely intended to go out all the time. Wait, though. Supposing he'd only popped out for something at the wrong moment—just as he had the night before? Sarah went looking for his favourite corner shop.

There was no mistaking it, and there were several shoppers there but Rory wasn't one of them. What to do now? Rory had praised the deli counter so she would buy something for her supper. The canteen would close long before she got back to the hospital.

The man Sarah thought must be Ali put all her purchases in a plastic carrier bag and asked if she was new to the district as he hadn't seen her before.

'No, just visiting,' she answered. 'A friend of mine who lies nearby was praising your shop, so I thought I'd drop in for a few things.'

'That is very nice,' he said, looking pleased. 'May I ask your friend's name? I pride myself on knowing all my regular customers.'

'Drummond. Rory Drummond,' obliged Sarah.

By the way that Ali's face lit up she realised that the admiration was mutual. 'You've just missed him,' said the shopkeeper. 'He was here with his girlfriend not fifteen minutes ago, picking up his paper.' He chuckled. 'Perhaps I should have said one of his girlfriends. He is very popular.'

'He certainly is,' agreed Sarah, hoping she didn't look and sound as cross as she felt. 'But, there, some of us have it and some haven't. Can you change a twenty?'

'No problem—and I'm sure the doc will be very sorry to have missed *you*, young lady, if you don't mind my saying so.'

'I do believe you're even more of a charmer than

he is,' Sarah told Ali with a brilliant smile as she took her change.

It was a safe bet that Rory would get to hear of this—and it served him right! Quiet, lonely evening all by himself, indeed! What kind of a fool did he think she was? And now where was the nearest ruddy bus stop?

Sarah gave the canteen a miss at lunchtime the next day. If Rory wanted to see her, he could damn well take the trouble to come and find her. But it was late afternoon before he sought her out, finding her in the doctors' room on her own wards.

'You look tired, darling,' he said, sounding quite concerned. 'Did you have an awful night?'

He could say that again, though it hadn't been for the reason he thought. 'I've known worse,' she answered. 'What about you?'

'Nothing special. As a matter of fact, I spent the evening with an old friend—but I'd much rather have been with you.'

'Oh, I'm sure you would! Some old friends are frightful bores, are they not? I was just about to have a coffee. Want one?' She got up to plug in the kettle and spoon coffee granules into mugs, careful to keep her back to him because of a ridiculous desire to burst into tears.

'What's up, Sary?' he asked perceptively.

'Nothing's up. What makes you think that?'

'You're putting up the shutters again, unlike Sunday...'

'There's a time and a place for everything and this is where we work. Did you know that dear old Charlie Greig died yesterday?'

'Yes, Jack Kinnear told me at lunchtime. I'm sorry. I liked him, too. But please, don't change the subject again, Sarah.'

'Sorry. One sugar or two?'

He ignored that to ask urgently, 'What's eating you, Sarah?'

'I don't know what you mean,' she dissembled, holding out his coffee.

He took both steaming mugs from her and set them aside. Then he took her by the shoulders, obliging her to look at him. 'If you're regretting Sunday and if you want to go back to being just good friends, then that's how it'll have to be, but— Oh, Sarah! I really thought we'd got beyond that. Still, if that's all you want—are prepared to give...' The pressure on her shoulders suggested he wanted her to deny that.

As so often with him, she found herself wondering how to get it right. 'You're a right puzzle, Rory Drummond,' she said at last as coolly as she could manage. 'I'd have thought you had all the girlfriends you could handle without taking on another!'

'None I wouldn't be happy to part company with if you...if you...' He'd run out of words. Or courage. Or cheek—or all three!

'If I came across?' she suggested bluntly.

Rory frowned, disliking the way she'd put it. 'I'm very, very fond of you, Sarah,' he admitted. 'And I'd begun to think you were quite fond of me...'

Fond. It was a word people used when they meant something—or next to nothing. 'I'll admit to slightly fond,' she said, 'but you're still the aggravating so-and-so you always were!'

He released her with a rueful grin. 'That's rather

how I feel about you some times,' he said. 'So when are we going out again?'

'I'm off tonight, but you're not, are you?'

'Tomorrow, then? Come to the flat tomorrow!'

She looked thoughtful because neutral ground might be safer till she'd gauged the opposition. 'How about…a drink and a film. Or something?' she was saying when the phone rang. She picked it up and listened, before handing it to Rory. 'Peter Blair,' she said.

Rory listened, his eyebrows climbing skywards. 'Would you believe it?' he breathed. 'Our consultant only thinks he's gone and given himself a Colles' fracture!'

'How?' asked Sarah but he was halfway down the corridor by then.

She poured away the unwanted coffee, then washed the mugs and tidied the desk, her mind busy elsewhere. Last night she'd worked herself into a right old lather because Rory had been out with somebody else. Today, his matter-of-fact explanation had calmed her down somewhat. She simply must learn to trust him—stop needling him all the time—or this second chance would slip away from her.

But, oh, Lord, how difficult it was to be sensible when your deepest emotions were involved…

'Where were you last night?' demanded Rory without so much as a good morning when he and Sarah met by chance next morning outside the path lab.

'I was out with an old friend,' she was able to say, having met Fiona in town again. 'Just as you were on Monday!'

'There's no need to be defensive—I was only wondering, that's all. You were out when I rang.'

Sarah didn't realise she'd sounded defensive. 'Just explaining,' she said. 'And it was nice of you to ring. Or has there been a hitch?'

'*Now* what's she got in her head?' asked Rory, gazing at the ceiling for inspiration.

'Oh, just wondering if, with your Mr Murray having hurt his wrist, you weren't going to be free tonight—that's all.'

'I *am* free tonight so our arrangement still stands—if that's all right with you.'

'Why wouldn't it be?' asked Sarah.

'How do I know? I've given up trying to fathom you.' He sounded genuinely puzzled.

'Then let me recap,' she suggested. 'We arranged to spend this evening together—or so I thought. I hope I'm not wrong, because I was rather looking forward to it.'

'I'll hang on to that,' he said. 'It's the most encouraging thing you've said to me since you woke up on Sunday morning. I should be able to get away by half-six. Pick you up outside the residence. OK? The forecast is for showers later.'

'Thank you—you're very thoughtful, Rory.'

'I do try—but I'd better get on. The boss is waiting impatiently for the reports I've come to collect.' He looked suddenly very serious. 'And, Sarah—I meant what I said, you know,' he told her as he shouldered his way into the lab.

Sarah frowned after him. He'd said all sorts of things in the past few days, so what precisely had he been referring to then? Perhaps she'd find out tonight. Meanwhile, there was work to be done.

'Guess who's first on your list this afternoon,' said the outpatient records clerk, coming in and dumping a formidable pile of case notes on Sarah's desk.

There was only one of their patients who caused a universal sinking of the heart. That dedicated smoker and ostrich... 'Hamish McWhirter,' Sarah sighed.

'You've got it—and I don't know why you don't wash your hands of him.'

'Because Dr Marshall says we must keep on trying to get through to him for the man's own sake.'

'Very noble—only it's not Dr Marshall doing the trying, is it?' asked the girl.

Sarah was sure she'd told him to come back in a month, so what was he doing here again so soon? She wondered no longer when he was wheeled in and she saw the swollen, discoloured left foot with its blackened toes.

'Heavens! What have we here?' she asked, bending down for a closer look.

'The wife,' he began. 'The daft besom dropped a can of baked beans on ma foot. I telt the doctor what did it so I dinna ken why he's sent us here.'

'A can of beans couldn't possibly have done that much damage. The circulation is very seriously impaired, as we told you—'

'They say whisky's the best thing for that, only it's that dear I'll need to get it on the National Health.'

You really have to admire his cheek, thought Sarah as she felt for the pulses in the arteries supplying blood to the lower leg and foot. As she'd expected, those to the foot were absent and the popliteal artery behind the knee was barely perceptible. She bit back the lecture she badly wanted to give and said, 'I'm going to ask Dr Marshall to take a look at you today, after which he will almost certainly refer you urgently to a surgeon. Those toes will have to be removed at the very least—possibly the whole foot.'

Had she been too brutal in giving that news? Sarah decided she probably had, but Hamish McWhirter never took in anything he didn't want to hear. Besides, his GP would have told him already.

'Dr Marshall will have to see Hamish today,' she told the nurse in charge. 'The silly old chap is for the chop now—literally!'

It was a big clinic that afternoon but, whether their problems were serious or slight, none of Sarah's other patients was as resistant to advice as her first one.

Bill Ferguson caught her just as she was tidying her desk afterwards. 'I hope you're not forgetting that you're on tonight, Sarah,' he said.

She stared at him, unable to believe his cheek. 'Since when?' she asked.

'Since we swopped on Monday.'

'Surely, if that was a swop, it was Monday for Sunday.'

'You're on tonight,' he repeated.

Sarah picked up the phone and rang Dr Cairns to clarify the situation.

'Look here, there's no need for that,' he blustered, as soon as he realised what she was doing.

She ignored him, said her piece to the senior registrar and then handed him the phone, saying, 'Dr Cairns wishes to speak to you.'

The look he gave her then was frankly murderous, and Sarah knew she'd made an enemy. But there were limits to her patience and the sooner he realised that, the better.

Besides, she had more important things on her mind, such as what to wear tonight—and was there time to do something about her hair?

CHAPTER EIGHT

SARAH took out her heated rollers and brushed her long, dark hair into a shiny, swinging cloud. Rory had admired her hair on Saturday, but things between them had gone downhill somewhat since then. Naturally, that was Rory's fault, for doing and saying things that made her doubt him. His subsequent plausible explanations should have been reassuring, but hadn't been.

He was taking her out tonight, though, so that had to mean some degree of enthusiasm... It's up to me to meet him halfway at least, she resolved. So she dressed with care in the outfit she'd worn for dinner at the Weavers' Arms and hurried down to greet Rory with what she hoped was a warm and welcoming smile.

'You look absolutely fabulous,' he said as he handed her into the car. Despite the teeming rain, he had got out to open the car door for her.

Sarah watched him dash round to the driver's side and get back in. There were dark, wet spots on his jacket and raindrops were clinging to his eyelashes and his thick untidy hair. 'You're very wet, Sir Galahad,' she said.

'I doubt I'll dissolve—just in case you're worried.'

'Nothing is worrying me tonight. I'm being taken out by an old friend of whom I'm...quite fond. And I'm really looking forward to my evening.'

He grinned down at her and said, 'After that, so am I.' As they set off he said, 'The police have found my car.'

'Where, Rory? And is it all right?'

'In a multi-storey car park in Stirling. The thieves had broken a window in order to gain access, but apparently there's no other damage. A clear case of desperation after being stranded, as we thought.'

'If you say so, but we didn't look round for a car to pinch when they'd stranded *us*, did we? Sometimes you're far too forgiving and easygoing, Rory.'

'Another bouquet? That makes two tonight and we've only just got to the main gate.' He was peering out through the driving rain to spot a break in the traffic. 'I'd not have been so forgiving if they'd wrecked it, though,' he went on, when they were out on the road and heading towards the city. 'I've not finished paying for it yet. But, there...'

'But there what, Rory?'

'I have good reason to be grateful to them.'

'How do you make that out?' asked Sarah sceptically.

'If the car hadn't been nicked, we'd not have stayed Saturday in Aberfoyle.'

'That's true,' she agreed, wondering what was coming next.

'And if we hadn't stayed away, we might not have discovered so soon that we're actually...quite fond of one another.'

Soon for him perhaps, but Sarah had known how she felt about him almost since the day they'd met. 'I see now what you're driving at—so all's well that ends well, then.'

'What do you mean, *ends*?' he demanded. 'As far as I'm concerned, we're hardly begun.' He swore as the windscreen wipers of the borrowed car packed up, sparing Sarah the need to find a suitable answer.

'We've just passed a call-box. Shall I dash back and call the AA?' she offered, but Rory said he thought they could manage if he hopped out occasionally to sponge the windscreen now that the rain was easing off.

That worked, after a fashion, but they were later getting to town than Rory had intended. Sarah knew that he lived out beyond the West End, but by now it was obvious that they were headed in the opposite direction and she wondered where they were going.

As though reading her thoughts, Rory said, 'My first idea was to take you straight home and dazzle you with my wonderful cooking, but I didn't think it would be a good idea so I'm making for that nice little Italian place.'

Sarah discovered that she was sorry about that, which was daft. 'Great, but is their cooking as good as yours?' she asked.

'You're joking,' he said as he got out to unlock the gates of his private parking area. By now the rain had eased to a drizzle.

Perhaps it was the weather, but the trattoria was half-empty tonight and they were served in record time. 'No, nothing else, thanks,' said Rory, when they'd put away large plates of spaghetti carbonara. 'We're having coffee at home.'

Sarah liked the way he'd said 'home' so naturally, and she tucked her arm through his for the walk back to the car. 'Careful,' he warned, his brown eyes glinting. 'If you're too friendly, I might get cheeky and Take Advantage.'

'Never mind—I'll know how to cope,' she murmured, to which he said that was what he was afraid of, showing that he hadn't understood what she'd been trying to tell him. Ah, well. The evening was young...

'Now this is what I call a flat,' enthused Sarah as she stepped into the spacious hall and saw the wonderful Victorian frieze and cornices, freshly repaired and repainted.

'Too often the soundproofing in modern flats is suspect, and I don't like hearing my neighbours slicing bread,' Rory said whimsically. 'You could hold an orgy in here and nobody would notice.'

'And how many orgies have you held so far?' Sarah asked promptly.

'Only a few,' he replied, grinning. 'They're too expensive, as well as messing up the place. Now, let me show you the rest of it.'

In swift succession he threw open doors to a fair-sized sitting room with rows and rows of books and an enormous sofa, a small sparsely furnished spare room, his own room, dominated by a large double bed, a bathroom, of course, and so to the last room. Its ceiling had been lowered, making it seem bigger. One end was a high-tech kitchen and the other housed a large pine table and chairs.

'It's lovely, Rory, really lovely,' praised Sarah. 'And just what I'd choose. To buy—when I've got a permanent job,' she added hastily, in case he thought she was hinting at moving in.

'Talking of which, have you—?'

'Written to the Dean? Yes—and he should get the

letter today.' She wrinkled her nose. 'What's the betting that he's forgotten me?'

Rory was at the sink, filling the kettle. Having switched it on, he turned round. His expression was thoughtful and questing. 'I doubt that,' he said. 'You're…fairly memorable, you know.'

'No, I didn't know,' Sarah returned hopefully.

'Then you'll just have to take it from me.' He loped across to the fridge and took out a magnificent hazelnut gateau.

'Oh, Rory—how wonderful! My absolute all-time favourite.'

'I know,' he said, pleased at her obvious pleasure.

'Rory, you're such a dear…'

'Just because I've remembered what you like to eat?'

'Not exactly…'

'Then tell me!'

'Oh, look, the kettle's boiling,' she said, unwilling to be the one to take the next—significant—step forward. Better to travel hopefully than arrive—and find she was only one of many!

'Jolly good,' Rory said woodenly. 'The one thing I crave most in the world just now is a nice cup of coffee.'

Sarah watched him fill the cafetière and put it on the tray, knowing that she'd disappointed him. And knowing, too, that by now she could have been flirting effortlessly with almost anybody else.

'I'll take the tray, if you'll bring the cake, and then we'll sit down at either end of the sofa and have a nice chat about work and the weather,' said Rory in the same lifeless way as before.

'I just can't seem to strike the right note with you,

can I?' She sighed as she followed him to the sitting room, where a long coffee-table waited in front of the sofa.

'You're not alone in that,' he answered. 'I'm not at my sparkling best either right now. The truth is, I'm not at all sure what you want of me. I thought I did first thing on Sunday morning, but since then you've gone all remote and mysterious on me.'

'Shy,' she whispered. 'Would you believe that I'm feeling kind of shy?'

His face lit up with a fierce eagerness as he said, 'Things are really looking up if Sarah Sinclair is feeling shy!'

'I hope you're not laughing at me,' she pleaded, just as the phone rang.

'No, Sarah, I'm not laughing at you,' he promised. 'I take you much too seriously for that.'

The phone went on ringing, and when he didn't move she asked, 'Are you not going to answer it?'

'I'm not on call, and as far as anybody else is concerned I'm out.'

'How strong-minded you are! I can never resist answering.'

'I know,' he said. 'And look where it got you on Sunday afternoon.'

'They knew I was in the hospital so I'd have been caught eventually. Why do you not have an answering machine?'

'I have, but it's on the blink.' He leaned forward and asked firmly, 'What was I saying to you when we were so rudely interrupted?'

'Something about taking me seriously…'

'Very seriously,' he corrected.

'Yes, I remember. And I think—'

'You're talking too much again and driving me slowly but surely up the wall!' He got to his feet and pulled her up by the elbows, drawing her close and searching her face for clues. 'Old mates—or something more?' he asked at last. 'It's your choice.'

The right words wouldn't come, but she was answering him wordlessly with her eyes.

'I— Oh, God,' she whispered as his arms went round her, drawing her quivering body close. Then he began to kiss her—forehead, cheeks, throat, before claiming her mouth. Desire coursed through her. *I never knew how it could be. I never knew... If this is what he means by quite fond—*

'My God, Sarah,' he breathed. 'Why did I never realise how wonderful you are?'

'Too close? Oh, I don't know!' She didn't want a debate, and to hell with caution—she'd loved him too long for that. Now all she wanted was to give herself completely to the love of her life.

Rory kissed her again with hungry longing. 'Sarah?' he asked hoarsely, and she nodded.

He took her hands, drawing her out of the room to the one with the big bed, where he undressed her with a skill and care that drove her wild. She found herself unbuttoning his shirt just as eagerly, unzipping his chinos, her patience tested to the limit. When they fell onto the bed, Sarah pulled him to her with fierce energy. This wonderful moment had been so long in coming... And then at last the pent-up passion of years erupted in a great explosion of joy.

Next morning, Sarah wakened after a wonderfully deep and dreamless sleep. She felt relaxed and peaceful, although she did wonder sleepily why the bed seemed so much bigger and more comfortable than usual.

When she heard the sound of running water and a beloved voice singing, memory came rushing in. She was in Rory's bed after the most wonderful, the happiest night of her life. She stretched luxuriously, savouring the memory. She was, without a doubt, the happiest woman in the entire world.

Soon after, the sounds of running water and singing stopped and Rory came in, towelling himself dry. Seeing that Sarah was awake, he dropped down on the bed to kiss her. 'Morning, angel. Did you sleep well?' he asked.

She smiled up at him and murmured, 'Like a log.'

'Not quite. Logs are quiet.'

'Are you saying that I snore?'

'No—but you do make little mewing noises like a lost kitten. Rather sweet, I thought. Now, I don't want to rush you, but we do have a hospital to go to. Remember?'

'I think I'll do a Bill Ferguson and pretend to be ill,' she decided jokily.

Rory pretended to be shocked. 'Good doctors don't do that,' he reproved with a comical scowl. Then he found her clothes and tossed them to her.

'Ugh! Yesterday's undies,' she said, wrinkling her nose.

'I could lend you a pair of boxers, if you don't think— No, wait! Chloe keeps a few things here…' He ambled off, stark naked.

Sarah shot up in his bed, feeling as though she'd just been treated to a cold shower. How many more of his women did she not know about? 'Who's Chloe?' she demanded, her eyes glinting, when Rory came back. She was much too wound up to be moved by a full-frontal view of his wonderful body.

He dropped some briefs and a pair of tights on the bed. 'A cousin of Mum's. Her work takes her away a lot, so she often dosses down here if she has to catch an early plane.'

Sarah held up the scanty lacy briefs between two disapproving fingers. 'Not quite what I'd have expected a contemporary of your mother's to wear!'

He laughed as though she'd made a joke. 'Old Chloe's nearer my age than Mum's,' he explained, making it worse. 'Now do get up, my flower, or you'll not have time for a shower *and* breakfast.' He dressed himself with all possible speed and went off, humming as he buttoned his shirt.

Sarah glared after him. How *dared* he be so cheerful and switched off when she was still feeling all soft and soppy?

He was right about time being short, though, so she also showered and dressed quickly, slightly comforted on finding that the briefs were too big. At least she'd got a better figure than his so-called cousin!

For breakfast he gave her five-minute porridge, scrambled eggs, hot toast and some very good coffee. 'You can cook after all, then,' she allowed. 'Last night I thought you were chickening out when you took me to that Italian place!'

Rory looked wounded. 'Would I lie to you?' he protested.

'I hope not,' she said. 'I wouldn't like that at all.'

His smile faded as he tuned in to her mood at last.

'Something's wrong, Sarah. Please, don't say you're having regrets.'

She decided that there was nothing to be lost by being candid. 'You'd better believe that I've not got much experience in such matters, but the way you're acting seems more like the morning after a one-night stand than—than a big step forward in a—a long-term friendship. That's all!'

His face was a picture of shocked innocence and he set down his cup with such a clatter that coffee went all over the table. 'Don't you understand anything at all?' he asked at last. 'I *have* to keep it light—or make love to you again. And there simply isn't time.'

'I'm sorry,' she mumbled in a strangled little voice. 'I thought I'd been—a disappointment.'

'If you have, it's not because of your response last night. For me, last night was everything I'd ever dreamed of. Now, for heaven's sake get a move on,' he begged briskly. Was he regretting having said so much? 'We've got about twenty minutes for a half-hour journey.'

'Ready when you are,' she insisted, jumping up from the table and running to find her jacket.

When they parted at the hospital she kissed her fingertips and pressed them to his mouth, before saying lightly, 'See you at lunch, then, my hero.' Then she dashed up to her room to put on some working clothes.

'You're late, Doctor,' teased Jack Kinnear when Sarah burst into his office.

'I know, and I apologise, your honour. I'm afraid I overslept. Have I held you up?'

'Not at all! The unit's fairly quiet until the next batch of admissions—though it's my guess you'll not get the blessed St Coull to admit as much.'

His name for the UNO never failed to amuse Sarah and she giggled. 'Are you not forgetting that she's off today?'

'That accounts for your bubbly mood this morning,' Jack decided.

Ah, Jack, if you only knew! 'So, what cases are we getting in today, then?' she asked.

Jack glanced at the list. 'A query, query, late onset multiple sclerosis, a long-term diabetic to be stabilised and a heavy smoker with a couple of gangrenous toes. He's for the vascular surgeons—only we've got a bed and they haven't.'

'Hamish McWhirter,' breathed Sarah. 'I can't wait to see how you deal with him.'

'Sounds as though I can expect a challenge,' returned Jack, unruffled, to which Sarah replied that he didn't know the half of it.

The patient with the neurological problem was the first to be admitted, which meant that Sarah had time to give him his admission examination before lunch. As these things went, his symptoms were quite mild, but to a man who'd never previously had a day's illness in his life, seeing double, having stiff, disobedient muscles and double his usual number of trips to the loo was very alarming. He would need a lumbar puncture to obtain some cerebrospinal fluid for analysis, but Dr Gray was off again today and Sarah had the other arrivals to clock in, as well as the usual routine ward work.

'What's the result, then, Doctor?' asked the patient, breaking in on her feverish programming.

Sarah explained that there were tests to be done and the consultant would be explaining everything to him once all the results were to hand. Then she wondered, as so often before, how she would cope if she ever became a consultant, and the buck stopped with her.

With that thought came another. How would a consultancy fit in with being a wife and a mother? Slow down, Sarah—this thing with Rory has only just begun. Remember all the other hopefuls on his list...

Because of her longing to see Rory, the morning seemed longer than usual, despite a heavy workload. Neither Rory nor Peter came to the canteen at lunchtime, though. With their chief in plaster, they must be extra busy, Sarah told herself. The poor man wouldn't be able to operate for a start!

When would she see Rory again? She was on duty tonight and he would be on at the weekend, having swopped so that they could go walking last Saturday.

Some of her questions were answered when he rang her unit, catching her between jobs in the late afternoon.

'Have you missed me?' he began.

'Would you believe as much as you've missed me?' she asked, thrilled to be hearing his voice for the first time since early morning.

'That'll do,' he said, with evident satisfaction.

'Does that mean you'll be coming to keep me company between calls tonight, then?' she asked hopefully.

'Believe me, there's nothing I'd like better,' he insisted, 'but there's something that must be done tonight, that I've been shirking for—too long. Now, about the weekend,' he dashed on before she could ask what it was. 'Do you want to come and stay at the flat?'

Didn't she just? 'But I thought you were on call.'

'So I am, but that doesn't mean I have to be in the hospital all the time—just at the end of a phone. Remember, there's no A and E department here.'

'I shall pack my bag tonight in case there's no time tomorrow,' cried Sarah.

'She's eager. I really like that,' purred Rory.

'You bet she's eager. Eager to escape this place!' Even as she said that, Sarah was wishing she could squash this lingering instinct to play safe.

'What else?' asked Rory with mock sadness. 'I'm just so glad to be able to oblige. Coming!' he called in answer to a summons at his end of the line. 'Sorry, Sary, love—I have to go now. See you!'

'Thanks for calling,' she said, a split second after he'd rung off.

They didn't meet at all next day, and when Rory eventually phoned, Sarah expected him to tell her what time to be ready. Instead, he said, 'Sarah, love, I'm at the City Hospital, would you believe? And I've no idea what time I'll get away.'

'What on earth are you doing there?' she asked, puzzled.

'They're on standby this weekend and that's invariably hectic, so the Prof in his wisdom has decided that from now on I'll be doing my duty weekends here, rather than at the Allanbank.'

'Can he do that?' Sarah asked foolishly, out of disappointment.

'Of course he can! And I'm surprised he hasn't thought of it before. It makes good sense.'

'I suppose it does,' she agreed reluctantly. 'Ah, well, I hope you'll not be too busy—and don't worry about me. I can always go and see Bruce.'

'You'll do nothing of the sort, I hope! Just so long as you don't mind going to the flat under your own steam, as there's no way I can get out there to collect you. The nice old boy who lives in the ground-floor flat keeps my spare key and I've told him you'll be calling for it. Make yourself at home and I'll come home any spare moments I get.' He laughed briefly. 'Not exactly the weekend I'd planned for you, but better than being marooned out in the sticks, I hope.'

'Much better, but— Oh, Rory! What a terrible disappointment!'

'It's almost worth being shanghaied by this place just to hear you say that,' he said. 'And the taxi's on me, sweetie—but I'm afraid it's *au revoir* for now.'

As Sarah hung up, the houseman appeared at her side. 'I was going to ask you to listen to Mrs Watson's chest,' he said diffidently, 'but I guess you're anxious to get away as you're off this weekend.'

'Not as keen as I was before that call.' She sighed. 'And, besides, work always takes priority. What seems to be the trouble?'

'A funny sort of swooshing noise—like a leaky heart valve, only not quite.'

'I don't like the sound of that,' said Sarah, lengthening her stride. She'd listened to Mrs Watson's chest that very morning, hearing nothing out of the ordinary. What could have happened?

'Try my stethoscope,' she told the houseman kindly, having listened in again.

He did—for some time, before handing it back to her. 'It's gone,' he said. 'I don't understand.'

Sarah led him away from the patient's bed. 'Check yours over,' she suggested. 'Either there's something blocking it, or there's a small cut in one of the tubes.'

'I did wonder,' he said, 'only they always say it's only bad workmen who blame their tools.'

'Better to be safe than sorry,' Sarah said with a smile. 'Never be afraid to ask for a second opinion. See you on Monday.'

It was five o'clock on Sunday afternoon and so far the weekend had been a non-event, romantically speaking.

On Friday Rory had come home at midnight, only to be called out again less than half an hour later. When he'd returned at four a.m. Sarah had been sleeping, and when she'd woken at eight he'd already been up and dressed.

'Somebody likes his work,' she'd said, yawning.

'Also well programmed,' he'd told her wryly. 'Saturday at the City is always a killer.' Then he'd dropped a kiss on the end of her nose and dashed off.

It had been on Sunday before she'd seen him again and then he'd literally fallen into bed and slept until two. He'd just had time to eat the late brunch she'd prepared for him before he'd been called in to the results of a multiple pile-up on the M73.

That was getting on for three hours ago and only an idiot or an incurable optimist would have been sitting by the window like this, watching for his return.

Sarah decided that she was neither so she went to the kitchen to make a pot of tea. Before the kettle had boiled she heard his key in the lock and ran to greet him.

She fetched up, stunned, in the doorway, because it wasn't Rory there, hanging up an expensive suede jacket, but an incredibly beautiful and elegant female, wearing the briefest possible skirt and with the longest and most wonderful legs that went on and on for ever. Her jacket disposed of, she picked up an overnight bag and swayed into the bathroom, humming a tune and kicking the door shut behind her.

Now, who the hell is she? wondered Sarah as she slumped against the doorpost. Not the cleaner, for sure—not on a Sunday and dressed in such clothes. She had her own key, though—the spare one was in Sarah's own handbag. The kettle boiled and Sarah made the tea with hands that shook. Then she sat down at the kitchen table, facing the door and waiting to see what happened next.

When she eventually appeared, the stranger was wearing Rory's dressing-gown, and the towel she'd wound turban-fashion round her head only added to her glamour. 'Hello,' she said chattily when she saw Sarah. 'So how do you fit in?'

'I'm an old friend of Rory's from student days.' That was as much as Sarah felt able to admit to.

'Ah—that one,' the unknown responded slowly and thoughtfully. Then she took a mug from the dresser and poured herself some tea.

Sarah found her composure both depressing and

infuriating. But if Rory has told her about me...
'Yes, we go back a long way,' she went on, 'and
now that I'm working in Glasgow again...' But why
should I be the only one to do the explaining? 'How
about you?' she asked, meaning, Where do you fit
in?

'Oh, here and there—but mostly in London. And
Paris.' Had she really misunderstood, or was she
very clever? 'Incidentally, Rory's on call this weekend, so there's no telling when he'll be home. If you
give me your number, I'll get him to call you. That
has to be better than hanging around here.'

Yes, she's clever all right—and determined to get
rid of me, Sarah realised grimly. 'As it happens, I'm
spending the weekend here,' she retorted levelly.
Though for all she'd seen of him... And now, with
this one turning up...

'He's so good about putting people up,' purred
the woman. 'Too good, I sometimes tell him! If you
trained in Glasgow, though, there must be loads of
other folk you could be visiting, so do feel free to
ring round if you want. There's a phone on the wall
there, right behind you.'

'You're too kind,' said Sarah with heavy sarcasm,
'but, actually, I'd arranged my evening before you
turned up.' Then she forced herself to stand up un-
hurriedly and saunter out of the kitchen.

I'm a fool to let myself be ousted like this, she
thought as she packed her bag. It'd damn well serve
him right if he came home and found us both here—
and very likely pulling him to bits! How she wished
she had the bottle—or the lack of feeling—to stay
here and brazen it out. But she couldn't. She loved
him far too much to be able to carry off such a

scene. Especially when this unknown woman was so much at home and so sure of her ground.

So much for Rory's fervent claim to be ready to drop all his other girlfriends if she came across!

I must have been mad to believe that—even for a moment, Sarah told herself bitterly as she crept out of his flat.

CHAPTER NINE

SARAH walked round the corner, out of sight of
Rory's front windows, before she stopped to wonder
what she should do next. Mentally, she ticked off
the possibilities, with going straight back to the hospital last on the list.

When a call to Fiona went unanswered she tried
Carrie, who responded with a cry of delight. Robin,
it seemed, was also having a hectic weekend on call
and Carrie was lonely. 'But why are we nattering
on the phone like this?' she asked, having told all
that. 'I've got such tremendous news so, if you're
not on duty, why not come round now for supper?'

'That's the best offer I've had for ages,' Sarah
responded gratefully. Then she bounded out of the
call-box and hailed a cab.

'Have you come to stay?' joked Carrie when she
saw Sarah's bulky holdall.

How extra-bouncy she was. Her news must, indeed, be tremendous. 'I've been away for the weekend,' explained Sarah, which was true as far as it
went. 'And I decided to call and find out if you were
free, before going back to the hospital.'

Carrie's round, good-humoured face split in a
wide grin, but she poured Sarah a sherry before saying, 'Yes, you could say I'm free for the moment.
We've fixed the date for our wedding. Five weeks
from yesterday!' Her eyes were soft with happiness.

'Good heavens! You're not wasting any time, are

you?' cried Sarah, as she settled on the nearest chair. 'Come on, now—let me hear it all.'

'Here goes, then!' Carrie sat down, too. 'It'll be in Robin's brother's church, with Archie conducting the ceremony. And James will be best man—if he can get leave, which he's sworn to do.'

'That's really keeping it in the family! And will your sister be your bridesmaid?'

'Chief bridesmaid. As you know, we only intended to have Marie, but Archie's wee twins begged and begged and I hadn't the heart to say no.' Carrie chewed her lip for a second or two. 'I hope things are not going to snowball, Sarah, but you know what mothers are like. We only want a simple wedding. What's the point of spending a whole lot of money on incidentals? It's the ceremony itself that counts.'

'Absolutely!' agreed Sarah. 'It's your wedding, so stand firm. And you know you can count on Fiona and me for any help you need.' And surely, she thought, after today Rory will have the decency to stay away. Arrange to be on call or something... Pull yourself together, girl! Carrie's giving you one of her sideways looks. 'What about the reception, Carrie?'

'It'll be at the manse. We're getting caterers in, but there'll be a fair amount to do beforehand so Susan would be glad of a hand. Oh, Sarah! I do so love talking about our wedding! Do you mind?'

'Of course not, you clown! I want to hear everything.'

Carrie jumped up to hug her friend. 'And I promise faithfully to listen to you when your turn comes.'

'I'll hold you to that,' Sarah answered, as expected, and even forced herself to smile. 'But now tell me all the other gossip.'

As usual, Carrie had plenty to relate, but she saved the juiciest bit until they were sitting down to supper. 'Moira's getting married,' she announced, causing Sarah to choke with surprise on a mouthful of coleslaw. 'So who's the lucky man, then?' she asked when she'd recovered.

'Some computer-chip tycoon she met when he was in the private hospital, getting his varicose veins done.'

'How romantic,' murmured Sarah as Carrie rattled on about how Moira had decided it was high time she settled down—with someone other than Rory Drummond!

So Moira had taken herself out of the running, but there was still Dulcie and Long Legs—and heaven knew who else! 'There ought to be a law against men like Rory Drummond,' said Sarah with just the right degree of couldn't-care-less. 'But tell me more about Moira's intended, Carrie. Is he loaded? And, more to the point, does he know any other rich tycoons who are scouting around for wives?'

Carrie fell about laughing as she told Sarah what fun she was, which was very reassuring. The last thing Sarah wanted was for Carrie—or anybody else—to suspect what a fool she'd almost made of herself over Rory Drummond.

'He didn't like it, of course,' said Carrie.

'Who didn't like it,' wondered Sarah, preoccupied as she was with keeping her end up.

'Rory, of course. Apparently, he tried to make out that he'd been wanting to end their thing for some

time, only he couldn't think how to put it. Rory
Drummond, stuck for words! Can you credit such a
thing?'

Sarah had known it to happen but, as expected,
she said, 'Not very easily.'

'And men try to tell us it's only us girls who are
keen to save our pride. More trifle, Sarah? It's rather
good, if I do say so myself.'

'I think I could manage another wee spoonful,'
agreed Sarah, 'and then I'd better think about going
for the bus. They stop a bit earlier on Sundays.'
Vividly she recalled how, only last Sunday, she'd
been on a bus with Rory, and so happy…

'Rubbish!' declared Carrie, startling Sarah out of
her soppy thoughts. 'I'm taking you home. We
haven't had a session like this for so long, and
you're not cutting it short.'

So it was well after midnight before Carrie would
hear of Sarah leaving. Robin still hadn't come home
and Carrie was getting worried about him. 'He
works so hard, Sarah,' she said for quite the fourth
time. 'I hoped things would be better now that the
Prof has arranged for two registrars to be on duty at
weekends at the City, but this is quite the worst one
yet.'

Sarah just managed not to tell Carrie about the
pile-up on the M73, which would have given the
game away. 'That's why I'm calling a cab,' she said
instead, picking up the phone. 'Robin will be hoping
for a large dose of TLC when he does get home—
not a note on the kitchen table.'

No doubt, Rory would be looking for the same
treatment—*and* he'd be getting it. Would he even
notice that another female was in place since he was

last at home? 'How lucky you are to have found a
man like Robin,' said Sarah, out of that thought.

'Oh, I know,' answered Carrie, serious for once.
'Men like Robin are few and far between.'

She could say that again!

Next morning Sarah was helping the houseman with
the routine blood samples when a nurse came to tell
her that Dr Marshall wanted to see her in Outpatients.

Damn, thought Sarah. Rory had a clinic that
morning and she'd quite decided to postpone their
next crucial meeting for as long as possible. Of
course, that would give him longer to cook up a
likely story, but it would also give her longer to
build up her resistance. Thank heaven her time here
at the Allanbank was nearly up.

Once in Outpatients she scooted past the orthopaedic consulting rooms at a near run and reached
Dr Marshall's room unseen.

He greeted her with a friendly smile. 'Ah, Sarah,
there you are! Sit down, please.' He finished the
note he was making, before asking, 'This is your
last week here with us as SHO, is it not?'

'Yes, sir. Dr Taylor comes back to work on
Monday next.'

'And Dr Gray has finally admitted that she's not
coping and has agreed to take sick leave.'

'Very wise,' murmured Sarah.

'So, if you've not already fixed up another job,
we'd like you to take over as locum registrar. After
all, you've been doing quite half the work for
weeks.'

In any other circumstances Sarah would have

been delighted. As things were, her main object was to get as far as possible from Rory. But where would she go? 'How long would the locum last?' she asked carefully.

'A month—until the start of Avril Gray's maternity leave proper. Unfortunately, the cover for that was arranged before you came to us, but if you've not got another job lined up I'd take it as a personal favour if you'd stay until the end of August. And who knows, Sarah? By then we may have found you another suitable post.'

Well, beggars couldn't be choosers, could they? 'I'd be delighted to take that locum, sir,' she exaggerated for form's sake.

Dr Marshall then told her how pleased he was, as well as saying some very nice things about her skill and commitment. 'And now you'll be wanting to get back to the wards,' he ended by way of dismissal.

Sarah took the hint, thanked him again for his efforts on her behalf and then, very carefully, opened the door. There was still no sign of Rory and she got safely out of the department. Had she been mad to let herself in for another month here? Could she bear it? She needed the job, though, and given a bit of luck, surely something far away from Glasgow would turn up in the next five weeks or so.

Back on the unit it was all systems go. 'We've just admitted one of our regular asthmas in status, Jack Kinnear is having trouble with a man who's changed his mind about going to Theatre, and the ortho. registrar has rung twice, needing to speak to you urgently,' reported Sister Gordon. 'So take your pick.'

'I have—and in that order,' decided Sarah, 'so lead me to your asthmatic.'

The girl had already been given emergency treatment by the paramedics who'd brought her in, but she was highly emotional and it took Sarah some time to calm her.

'The trouble is, I've had to put her in the bed earmarked for Dr Marshall's new patient, Mrs Shaw,' confided Jean Gordon. 'And as the poor soul's already been cancelled once, I'd hate to have to cancel her again.'

Sarah thought swiftly. 'Mrs Barclay would have gone home last Friday if the daughter who lives with her hadn't decided to go off on holiday at the very last minute. But there's another daughter, living in Paisley, so why not get the medical social worker to bring a bit of pressure to bear there? After all, this is an acute unit for providing urgent treatment, not a respite care facility.'

'I like Mrs Barclay,' said Jean obliquely.

'So do I—and I can understand her daughter getting worn down by all the responsibility, but she's not going the right way about getting help. Try the MSW, there's a dear, while I go and deal with Jack's problem.'

Not unexpectedly, it was Hamish McWhirter who was having second thoughts about surgery. 'There must be something they could put on ma foot to heal it up,' he began the minute Sarah put her head round the curtain. 'I mean, choppin' it off is so kinda final.'

So is dying, if they don't, thought Sarah wryly. 'The blood supply has failed and the foot is past saving,' she explained yet again. 'It's just *got* to

come off, Mr McWhirter, before it poisons your
whole system. Surely you can understand that?'

'But they can do such great things these days,
Doctor. I was readin' in the newspaper about this
surgeon who sewed an arm back on after it was torn
off in an accident.'

'That was entirely different from your case,' protested Sarah. 'I'm not being unhelpful, you know. I
do realise how it must feel to be faced with losing
your foot but, believe me, losing the whole leg
would be a whole lot worse. And that's what it could
come to—and very soon—if you go on refusing to
face facts.'

She could see that he was boiling up for another
objection so she hurried on, 'And before you ask,
no, you cannot have a leg transplant. That would be
quite impossible. The man you mentioned had his
own arm sewn back on.'

'I ken that. D'you think I'm daft, lassie?'

'Not daft, but very obstinate, Mr McWhirter. So
do I send for the theatre porters or ring for a taxi to
take you home?'

'OK, you win,' he said grudgingly at last, and
Sarah whispered to Jack to give him his premed
quickly, before he changed his mind again.

'I'd like to meet the man who could out-talk you,
Sarah Sinclair,' said Jack, when he'd given the in-
jection. 'Meet him, and shake his hand. Oh, and before I forget, the ortho. reg. has been trying to reach
you since eight o'clock this morning.'

'Yes, I've heard, thanks. It's not—important. Is
there anything else you need me for before I start
trying to work out how not to have to put patients
two in a bed on the women's side?'

Jack said no, but if it would help he'd not mind putting a nice young lady in Hamish's bed, now that the vascular surgeons had found him a bed in their unit, post-op.

'I knew there had to be a silver lining somewhere,' responded Sarah.

'Then show it to me,' he called after her as she hurried away.

'No joy,' said Jean Gordon when Sarah looked round her office door. 'Mrs Barclay's other daughter isn't answering her phone, so the MSW's been onto the social work department who may be able to help, but not before Wednesday—and they'll need a doctor's say-so.' She handed Sarah a message slip with the number to ring.

'And they shall have it right away,' returned Sarah, laying her hand on the desk phone. It rang before she could pick it up. 'Never mind,' she said, 'I'll ring from the doctors' room.'

She regretted that decision as soon as she opened the door and found Rory there, waiting. 'The mountain has come to Mahomet,' he said grimly, planting himself between her and the door before she could bolt. 'What on earth got into you last night, running off like that without a word?' he demanded. 'Chloe—'

So *that's* who she was—his so-called cousin! And how dared he pretend that she, Sarah, was the one in the wrong? 'I got bored,' she said through stiff lips. 'Such a dreary weekend—so I went to see an old friend.'

'Until after one? I phoned three times last night and again on and off all morning. You must have known I'd be worried!'

There he went again! Everything was all her fault. 'I never dreamed you'd give it a second thought,' she said tautly. 'And it wasn't as if you came home to an empty flat. The first reserve turned up before I left!'

'Sarah, listen! You've got it all wrong!'

Did he really think he could still bamboozle her? 'No, Rory—*you* have! All right, so we've had some—some good times, but the price is too high for me, that's all. Simple as that.'

'Simple it bloody well is not!' he exploded. 'Will you listen to me for one minute?'

'I've listened to far too much from you already, Rory Drummond,' she said. 'And I don't want to hear any more—and that's final! Sorry,' she added absurdly.

If she hadn't known him so well, she could almost have believed that the pain in his eyes was real. 'Yes, you're sorry,' he charged harshly. 'Sorry for ever letting me near you! Why don't you be honest for a change, and admit as much?'

'While you, of course, are broken-hearted—because there's one woman in this world who's not taken in by you! Save the outraged innocence act for those who are. God knows, there are enough of them around, by all accounts. Now, please go. I've got work to do, if you haven't!'

If there had been pain in his eyes before, it had turned to contempt now. 'Don't worry—I'm going,' he snarled. 'I'm only sorry I ever thought you were worth bothering with!' Then he wrenched open the door and thrust out into the corridor.

Sarah stood as though turned to stone until his footsteps died away. Then, white-faced and trembling with reaction, she shut the door and wilted into a chair. Rory was the one who was cheating, surely she wasn't wrong about that, but as always he was the one who'd had the final word.

That's the last time I'll ever let a man get close to me, she resolved. They're double-dyed snakes, the lot of them. But— Oh, oh, Rory! Why did it have to turn out this way? Better that we'd never met again.

Two weeks later, Sarah locked up the tiny basement flat and ran up the steps to the two-year-old, genu-ine-low-mileage Nissan Micra parked at the kerb. She'd rented the first and bought the second on the strength of temporary promotion to registrar. But then she'd had to get out of hospital accommodation when the SHO job had ended and a car was a must for nights on call.

She had been locum registrar for a week now and the change had been seamless. As Dr Marshall had said, she'd been doing half the work anyway, and with the regular SHO back from sick leave she was having the easiest time she'd had since starting work at the Allanbank.

She needn't have worried about running into Rory either—it was now quite clear that he was as keen as she was to avoid meeting.

Rory. Well, what had she lost? Nothing. She was merely back where she'd always been with him. Nowhere. I'm being very sensible and practical these days, Sarah told herself as she joined the steady flow of traffic heading east.

Her new-found serenity received a jolt when she arrived at the hospital to find that the only space left in the car park was next to Rory's grey Audi. So what? All she had to do was make sure that he left before she did that night.

It was raining quite hard now and Sarah was rummaging under the driver's seat for her umbrella when she heard firm footsteps she recognised approaching. She crouched lower and waited.

Rory found whatever it was he'd forgotten and relocked his car, but he didn't move away. 'Are you stuck?' he asked after a minute.

There was nothing for it but to straighten up, scarlet and humiliated. 'I seem to have lost my umbrella,' Sarah admitted tightly.

'Try the parcel shelf,' he suggested curtly, before turning away.

Sarah watched him go; broad-shouldered, tall, athletic—irritating—before doing as he suggested. And, of course, the damn thing was where he'd spotted it. How could she have not seen it?

She locked her car and stamped off towards the hospital herself, cross at being wrong-footed like that but also all churned up inside by the look of him and the sound of his voice. And, worst of all, by the fact that he seemed totally unaffected by their first encounter since that awful row. So she was confirmed in her original reading of the whole situation, but that didn't make it any easier to bear.

But only a few more weeks to go. It felt like for ever.

On her desk in the doctors' room, Sarah found a letter from the Dean. It was brief and very much to the point. There would shortly be a vacancy for a medical registrar at Glasgow General Hospital, and if she cared to apply, he and Dr Marshall would be happy to support her application.

The General! There'd be lots of interesting cases, some lecturing to students, a chance for some research perhaps—and a real incentive to study for her MRCP. So why am I not over the moon? she wondered, even as she realised the reason. This was a golden opportunity to restart her career, but there was a distinct possibility that Rory could turn up there. It was Glasgow's biggest hospital, but was it big enough to hold them both?

She shrugged. Nothing in this life was quite perfect and she knew she would have to take that chance. Meanwhile, there was work to be done here—and more of it than usual, with Dr Marshall starting his summer holiday today.

'It's a big clinic today, Doctor,' Sarah was warned when she appeared in Outpatients.

'Never mind—I'm a big girl now,' she responded hardily.

But not big enough, apparently. 'I understood I'd be seeing a specialist,' said the first patient ominously.

'I've had a lot of experience with chest conditions, Mrs Pringle,' Sarah said encouragingly.

'But you're a woman!'

How about that for stating the obvious? 'Fifty per cent of doctors are nowadays,' Sarah pointed out.

'But not specialists.'

She had a point there. 'If you'd rather consult a man, that's your decision,' Sarah said quietly, 'but it will mean a wait of several weeks and your GP has asked particularly for an early appointment. So how about making do with me in the meantime?'

'Lot of fuss,' grumbled the patient, taking another line. 'There's nothing wrong with me that taking things a bit easier'd not cure.'

Fifteen minutes later Sarah was able to agree about the need for easing up, but not that there was nothing wrong. 'Do you cough up phlegm, Mrs Pringle?' she asked carefully.

'Aye—now and again. So does anybody.'

'And do you often wake during the night, sweating?'

'Oh, aye. But, then, it's summertime.'

'And you're always tired and often breathless.' That was a statement, not a question.

'Aye. Like I said, I'm needing a rest.'

After much persuasion and more muttered comments about fuss, Sarah managed to get Mrs Pringle to produce a sample of sputum and agree to a chest X-ray. She sealed the request form for that in an envelope. There was time enough for the patient to find out she had tuberculosis in the apical segments of both lungs when she was put on specific medication. There was no doubt about the diagnosis. Sarah had seen too many such cases among the immigrants who'd attended her clinic in southern Italy.

Mrs Pringle had seen her specialist after all.

Most of the patients that morning were new, and for most of them it was a matter of rubber-stamping the GP's diagnosis and arranging for the necessary hospital-based investigation and treatment. On her way to her own unit afterwards Sarah ran into Peter Blair.

Peter was in a chatty mood and oblivious to Sarah's anxiety to escape before Rory appeared. 'Long time, no see, Sarah,' said Peter.

'Mmm, yes. I've been pretty busy, one way and another.'

'We were awfully sorry that you couldn't come to our party.'

She felt she had to say, 'So was I, but I hear it was a great success.'

'It certainly seemed to go with a swing. We missed you, though.'

'You're awfully kind,' returned Sarah. But how could she have gone when Rory would have been there, flaunting whichever of his women had been flavour of the week?

'Are you on your way to lunch, Sarah?' Peter asked.

'Not yet—I've a million things to do on the unit first.' She smiled and moved away, but too late.

'I wish I had time to stand about, gossiping,' said Rory, right behind her. 'You must have finished early, Pete.'

'Yes, two of my patients didn't turn up. Some mix-up over transport, I gather.'

'Then you can come with me to see a chap on Coronary Care. He has an old, untreated fractured neck of humerus that's causing him some trouble…' He marched Peter away with a hand on his shoulder and without so much as a glance for Sarah. She felt dreadfully conspicuous. With people up and down the corridor all the time, such rudeness couldn't have gone unnoticed.

Or could it? Nobody was staring. I'm just too damn sensitive where he's concerned, she realised. I've got to learn to cope. Only three weeks to go. Oh, hell! What madness brought me back to Glasgow in the first place?

'What are we to do about this request from Orthopaedics for Dr Marshall to take over one of our old-timers?' asked Jean Gordon as soon as she saw Sarah. 'It seems that she's ready for discharge from their point of view, only—'

'They're not happy about letting her go, on account of her medical condition, but they want her bed,' said Sarah, who'd heard it all before.

Jean laughed and told her she was psychic.

Psychic? What a laugh. If she had been, she'd never have got caught in Rory Drummond's net! 'Did you tell them we don't have a bed?' asked Sarah.

'Of course I did, Sarah. And they said she's now a medical rather than an orthopaedic problem.'

Sarah wouldn't have said no to a tenner for every time this problem had cropped up since she'd come here. 'Did you tell them that Dr Marshall is on holiday?'

'No, but they must know from the usual memos going round. It's my guess that Mr Murray means to pull rank on a locum registrar.'

'He can try,' Sarah said firmly, 'but if we don't have a bed, that's that.'

'I'm afraid you'll have to tell him,' warned Jean. 'He flatly refused to take it from me.'

'But he'll have to take it from the head of the other medical unit, and Dr Graham is nominally in charge here during Dr Marshall's absence.' Sarah picked up the phone, ready to pass the buck.

'So what did Dr Graham say?' asked Jean hopefully when Sarah put it down again.

'That he's delighted to offer any medical advice

I may require, but he's perfectly happy to leave all administrative decisions to me.'

'The devious wee divil,' breathed Jean, echoing Sarah's own thoughts. 'So what will you do?'

'Go in search of Mr Murray.'

'He'll likely be at lunch now.'

'Just what I'm counting on, Jean. He can hardly tear me off a strip in the canteen.'

When Sarah eventually ran Mr Murray to earth in his office, Rory was with him. 'To what do I owe this pleasure, Dr Sinclair?' the consultant asked playfully. It was said that Mr Murray had an eye for the girls. Just like his registrar, thought Sarah grimly. No wonder they get on so well! 'Your patient, Mrs Brand, sir. You asked us to take her over, but I'm sorry to have to tell you that we can't. Our wards are full.'

Mr Murray pursed his lips thoughtfully, before deciding on retreat. 'Sort it out with Rory, there's a good girl,' he said smoothly. 'I have an urgent consultation at the Royal Infirmary.' Then he grabbed his jacket and briefcase and disappeared.

'It must be lovely to be a consultant and able to pull rank,' said Sarah bitterly, preparing to follow suit.

'We were told to sort out a problem,' Rory reminded her stonily.

'What is there to sort out?' she asked. 'You've got a patient you want to pass on to us, but we can't take her because we have no beds. End of story.'

'Perhaps you're not aware of the length of our waiting list,' she was told.

'And are all these waiting patients of yours emergencies?' Sarah asked crisply.

'You know very well that we only do elective surgery here,' Rory answered loftily, 'but that doesn't mean—'

'Precisely!' Sarah cut in. 'You do non-emergency work, whereas ours is an acute unit, taking emergencies. And that plays havoc with our own non-emergency admissions, let me tell you!'

'So you have got a bed!'

'No, we have not—and what will happen tomorrow when we're on standby for admissions, I really do not know.'

'There must be *one* patient you could discharge.'

'You're welcome to come and see for yourself if you don't believe me!'

'Don't be childish!'

'Childish, did you say? That's brilliant, coming from you.'

'And what is that supposed to mean?'

'As if you didn't know! Though, on second thoughts, permanent adolescent probably describes you better.'

'You've lost me,' Rory retorted in a very superior tone.

'How can anybody lose something they never had in the first place?' yelled Sarah, now quite at the end of her tether. Then she rushed out before she gave herself away completely.

That had been a near thing! She had nothing left now but her pride and she'd lose that, too, if Rory ever guessed how she really felt about him.

CHAPTER TEN

EVEN with Dr Marshall back from holiday, the clinic had taken most of the morning and then, just as Sarah was shutting the door after the last patient— as she'd thought—she was told about an extra patient. 'A Mr Hamish McWhirter—in a wheelchair.'

Sarah couldn't help smiling wryly. Hamish McWhirter had been her most awkward patient during her spell here at Allanbank Hospital, so it was appropriate that he should turn up on her last day. 'Right, then, let's have him in,' she responded.

The nurse had seen that smile and didn't approve of it. 'The poor man had to have his leg off after his wife dropped a curling stone on his foot and smashed it,' she said reprovingly.

'He told me it was a can of beans,' Sarah returned mildly.

'But, surely a can of beans couldn't do that much damage?'

'Certainly not,' Sarah agreed, 'which does make one wonder.'

'Wonder what?' asked the girl, clearly puzzled, so Sarah suggested gently she'd find that five minutes with the patient's notes after the clinic would be very enlightening.

'I want one o' they suction legs without a lot o' straps on it,' said Hamish when Sarah had asked how he was getting on.

'That'll be for the limb specialists to decide,' she

said firmly. 'But it's your chest I'm supposed to be looking at today. Your GP says in his note that your breathing has been worse since you got home from hospital.'

'Aye, it'll be yon anaesthetic for the op. It does that, ye ken.'

'Not if you have an intra-thecal—that is, a spinal anaesthetic, Mr Mac.' And she knew he had because of his chesty history.

'The gas gets into the lungs, though, don't it? Has to—whichever way they pump it in. Now what are ye daein', hen?'

'Helping you out of your sweater and shirt so that I can listen to your chest.'

'Help yourself,' he responded, plainly humouring her.

As well as the usual rales and rattle due to his chronic bronchitis, Sarah soon located the ominous dull patch which had prompted his doctor to refer him to hospital so urgently. Her lips compressed as she put away her stethoscope and reached for an X-ray request form. 'I think we should have a picture of that chest of yours,' she said. 'There seems to be a—a wee obstruction in your left lung.'

'It'll be the phlegm, Doctor. It's no' comin' up just as easy as it did afore the op.'

'Best to be quite sure, though, Mr McWhirter.'

'Ye're thorough, lassie. I'll say that for ye.'

'Only doing my job,' she responded gravely.

'Are ye no' goin' to tell us to give up on the ciggies the day?' he asked perkily as Sarah helped him dress again.

'Would you do it if I did?' she asked.

'Ye're learnin',' he said with a laugh that ended in a fit of coughing.

But sadly you haven't, thought Sarah, as the nurse wheeled him out. And now it's probably too late...

'Goodness me, lassie, I'd no idea you felt so badly about leaving us,' teased Dr Marshall from the doorway.

Sarah raised her head and managed a wan smile. 'I've just seen Hamish,' she explained, 'and he always leaves me feeling I'd be better in another sort of job altogether.'

'Go down that road and you'll end up as a patient yourself, Sarah,' warned the consultant. 'You must think positively. As long as our successes outnumber our failures—and they certainly do—then we're not wasting our time. Now come up to the unit with me. Miss Coull has got a little surprise for us.'

The surprise turned out to be a sandwich lunch in the UNO's office, along with the senior staff, followed by the presentation of a pretty piece of Caithness glass for Sarah to remember them by. This was a ritual not usually extended to locum staff and Sarah was suitably touched. She managed quite a pretty little thank-you speech and ended by saying that wherever she found herself working next, she was sure the staff couldn't possibly be any nicer than the ones she was leaving behind.

Then Dr Marshall asked if that was really the time? He'd been due at the General Hospital half an hour ago. 'And I'll be seeing you there at your interview on the twelfth, Sarah,' he called over his shoulder, before disappearing in his usual whirlwind fashion.

An hour or two later, when Sarah was making

notes which would be helpful to the incoming locum, Miss Coull appeared with the man himself in
tow. 'Can I leave him with you, Sarah?' she asked,
after introducing him.

Just as though he were a parcel, thought Sarah,
rising to her feet with a welcoming smile.

The newcomer gave her a look which was clearly
intended to captivate. 'Being at a loose end today, I
thought I may as well look in and get all the details
from you at first hand,' he explained in a charming
Irish lilt.

He was tall and dark and very handsome, and he
left Sarah absolutely cold. How long, she wondered,
before I can see a new man without comparing him
unfavourably with Rory?

'How thoughtful,' she said. 'You've just saved
me from a bad attack of writer's cramp. Let's go
round the unit and you can ask your questions as
the need arises.'

'You don't waste time, do you?' he asked as
Sarah reached for her white coat.

'Not if I can help it,' she returned.

It was amusing to see how swiftly he bowled over
Jean Gordon and the other female nurses. Naturally,
Jack Kinnear was unimpressed. 'Quite the charmer,'
he commented when Dr O'Connor left them for a
few minutes to take a phone call. 'You must be sorry
you're leaving us, Sarah.'

'Want to bet?' she asked, smiling.

'I only bet on certainties,' said Jack. 'Unfortunately, they don't always come off.' He eyed her so
knowingly that Sarah was sure he'd guessed about
her and Rory. She knew she was right when he said,
'I hope it's a success, girl—this job at the General.

Personally, I'd expected you to go for something…further away.'

Had he, indeed? 'Firstly, I haven't got the General job yet, and secondly, after four years away, I decided that there's no place like home.'

Jack accepted that and returned, 'The best place for a woman, if you ask me—and so I'm always telling Christine.'

That had to be a joke to cover Sarah's embarrassment. Jack's partner was a lawyer, bringing in at least twice as much as he was. So the awkward moment was glossed over in mutual laughter.

At least there'll be no need to suspect double meanings in my next place, Sarah comforted herself as Dr O'Connor returned and the hospital tour continued. Afterwards, he claimed not to remember the way to the car park, so Sarah showed him. She was waving him away in his highly conspicuous sports car when Rory came up to her.

'That your latest?' he asked curtly, jerking a derisive thumb towards the noisy car.

'That was Dr O'Connor, Dr Gray's permanent locum,' she said tightly. 'What a pity you were just too late to be introduced. He's just your sort—you'd have a lot in common.'

'Perhaps—perhaps not. I've never met a permanent locum.'

Sarah flushed. 'You know quite well what I meant,' she said crossly. 'He's the real locum. I was only standing in for a month.'

'Which is up.' He looked at her broodingly, before asking, 'So where are you going next?'

As if he cared one way or the other. 'On holiday,' she said shortly, before walking away.

'Then I hope it does you good. Straightens you out,' he called after her.

Sarah spun round fast. 'I'm not the one who needs straightening out,' she called back angrily, but too late. Rory was already shut in his car and revving the engine.

Too late. She was always too late with him. Vividly she recalled the day they'd met, just two of so many other eager youngsters more or less straight from school. It had been too late even then, if only she'd known it.

Sarah twisted this way and that in front of the long mirror in her tiny bedroom. She had put on a jacket and dress of soft cream silk jersey, years old but of timeless and classic cut. She'd lashed out on a new bag and shoes for the wedding, though. A large silk bow in peacock colours nestled in her upswept hair, doing duty as a hat.

She frowned at her reflection and thought, I look more like the bride's mother than her good friend. But she was already late so she'd have to settle for that.

Traffic was heavy that Saturday morning, making her later still, and most of the other guests had arrived by the time she was ushered into one of the front pews, reserved for close friends, by Carrie's young brother, important and unfamiliar in a dark, conservative suit.

Sarah took her seat beside Fiona, but not until a swift look round had failed to show her Rory's thick, unruly, dark thatch among the guests across the aisle. Having dreaded to see him, she was now unreasonably disappointed.

'Gosh, you do look nice,' Fiona whispered admiringly.

'So do you. That shade of blue really suits you,' Sarah whispered back.

'I got it specially, but it's not quite what I—' The organist struck a warning chord and an expectant rustle all around cut Fiona short.

Robin, stiff and self-conscious, stood up with his brother James. The oldest Tait brother, who would be taking the service, took his place in front of the communion table with what looked very like a reassuring wink for the groom. Shortly afterwards, Carrie sailed past on her father's arm, radiant and lovely in honey-coloured lace. Her sister and her two small nieces-to-be arranged themselves behind her. There was a stifled sob from the sentimental Fiona and the service began.

There was no mistaking the determined sincerity of the bridal couple's responses and their friends and relatives gave them every support with some lusty singing of the hymns.

'Wasn't it just beautiful?' asked Fiona, now openly weeping as Robin and his new wife went into the vestry with their attendants.

'Very moving,' Sarah agreed, although her attention had not been one hundred per cent on the ceremony. Rory wasn't there. Where was he and what was he doing? And he was supposed to be one of Robin's best friends. Perhaps he was working. Yes, that must be it. Sarah had forgotten hoping he would stay away.

'That pushy daughter of the Prof's is here with her parents,' reported Fiona, who had dried her eyes to look round and take stock. 'You know—the one who got so mad when you went outside with Rory at Carrie's and Robin's party.'

'Yes, I know who you mean. It's not surprising that she's here, though, is it? Being the Prof's one and only—as well as having worked with Robin.'

'Did you know that she was running after Robin before she latched on to Rory?' asked Fiona.

'Any port in a storm,' returned Sarah, who wished Fiona would talk about something else.

'What do you mean?' asked her puzzled friend.

'I hardly know,' Sarah admitted. 'Shh! Here they come. Doesn't Carrie look simply wonderful?'

She certainly did. Her eyes were brilliant and her smile wide, while Robin—relaxed and confident now—was gazing down on her as though he'd just caught a glimpse of heaven. Now it was Sarah's turn to shed a tear or two.

She didn't see Rory until they were all outside, clustered round the bridal group, while cameras flashed all around.

It was Fiona who spotted him first. 'He must have been even later than you, Sarah, and just slipped in at the back. I say! Dulcie's giving him a terrible glare. Do you suppose they've had a row?'

'She's probably peeved because he didn't go and sit with her and her parents.'

'That wouldn't account for such malice. Look at her.'

'I dare say you're right then, and they have had a row. Rory's very good at having rows with people.'

'But not with the Prof's daughter, Sarah. That wouldn't be sensible.'

'Well, then, perhaps she's found out about his

glamorous, so-called cousin who has her own key and comes and goes as she pleases.' God! I really must guard my tongue.

Fortunately, Fiona had just been greeted by Angus Forbes and had missed Sarah's last sentence. Sarah, in turn, was taken over by Moira and her fiancé. He was younger than Sarah had expected and not bad-looking either. Quite entertaining as well, and disposed to be very nice to his beloved's old university friend. He insisted on escorting them both to the manse for the reception.

By the time they were ready to move on to the desserts, Moira was openly restless. She'd only intended to show off her prize and then move on to dazzle others, yet here she was, stuck in a threesome with the only girl she'd ever really envied. When the best man came up to renew his acquaintance with Sarah, Moira seized the chance to edge her fiancé away from danger.

'You deserted me,' charged James, looking very soulful.

Sarah gazed at him, wide-eyed and puzzled.

'At that party in Robin's flat. You went off with that Rory Drummond character.'

Her expression cleared. 'Only to save my pride—after you left *me* for that gorgeous nurse.'

'I was only trying to make you jealous—and it seems I may have succeeded,' he purred, putting an arm round her shoulders.

'You certainly did—and I've not been the same girl since,' pretended Sarah, smiling coquettishly. How easy it was to talk provocative nonsense to any man who didn't matter. James was playing the game expertly, too, and she was almost sorry when his official duties took him back to the bridegroom's side for the formal part of the proceedings.

'You've not lost your touch, I see,' hissed Rory, taking James's place.

'Meaning?' asked Sarah with a lightning change of mood.

'Dazzling Moira's fiancé and re-attaching James Tait is pretty good going for one afternoon.'

'It certainly would be, if that was what I'd done.'

'Are you denying it?'

'Certainly. I was merely being polite.'

'Is that a fact? Then you'd better be careful not to be really encouraging, or you could start World War Three!'

'I don't know why you're bothered—you're quite safe from any such attention!' Oh, Rory, Rory, that's not at all what I meant to say...

'I know that,' he retorted. 'I was only issuing a general warning. Now, let's listen to the speeches.'

The speeches were witty, moving and also brief. Toasts were drunk and the happy pair began to mingle with their guests. By then, Rory had melted back into the crowd. Looking round for somebody else to talk to, Sarah came face to face with Dulcie Carlisle.

Dulcie was flushed, and rather drunk. 'Do you give lessons?' she demanded.

Sarah blinked, before asking, 'What sort of lessons?'

'In grabbing other girls' men—that's what! I've had my eye on you!'

'I'm very flattered,' Sarah told her.

'Oh, yes—very cool. But you've not done him any favours, you know! He'll never get another job

in Glasgow when he finishes at the Allanbank. My
father'll see to that. He always does what I want.'

A likely story on both counts.

'I have no idea what you're talking about,' insisted Sarah.

'I thought he'd volunteered for the Allanbank because we had a little tiff, but it was you, wasn't it?
He went there after *you*. Don't deny it!'

'You're drunk,' said Sarah, which was certainly
true.

'Not too drunk to see what's under my nose—and
it stinks! So there!' Apparently satisfied that she'd
made her point, Dulcie tottered off through the thin-
ning crowd, managing to cannon off several people
on the way.

Through a window, moments later, Sarah saw
Dulcie being roughly manhandled into his car by her
father. He looked murderous. Cross with her for getting drunk and showing him up, Sarah supposed in
passing, but her mind was principally busy with
what Dulcie had said, no matter how garbled it had
been. Where had she got the idea that Rory had
volunteered for the Allanbank because of me? He
couldn't have—he didn't know I was there. She's
got it all wrong. Best to forget her drunken ram-
blings.

But Sarah couldn't forget, because a pattern was
emerging. Dulcie, Moira, herself... One by one,
Rory was discarding his women. And all for blasted
Chloe. Who else?

After the happy couple had departed for a short
cruise to the Hebrides, those of the old crowd left
behind decided to end the day at their favourite pub
near the university. Having first made sure that Rory

wasn't among them, Sarah went, too, for the sake of appearances. Her mind was far away, though, and it was a relief when the pub closed and she was alone at last in her little car.

She left behind some very curious and puzzled friends. They couldn't ever remember Sarah Sinclair being so quiet and thoughtful before. They speculated for some time about it, without coming anywhere near the truth. Fiona, who half suspected, was careful to say nothing that could give them a clue.

Sarah checked in and went to sit in the departure lounge, having first removed her raincoat. It had rained almost all the time she'd spent in Surrey with her mother and her sister's family, while in Glasgow they'd been having a heatwave.

Her mind turned yet again to her interview for the job at Glasgow General Hospital in two days' time. She still hadn't decided whether or not she wanted it. Professionally, it would be splendid, but personally... Grow up, Sarah, she told herself firmly. If he does turn up there, it'll not be for months.

She glanced at the flight indicator board. Still no call and she'd been sure she'd missed the plane after that snarl-up on the M25.

Fifteen minutes later, the waiting passengers were told that the flight had been delayed by engine trouble, but that a relief plane was being prepared. In order to escape from the grumbles erupting all round her, Sarah went to get coffee from a machine. When she returned she found that her seat had been taken—by Chloe!

She backed off so hastily that she spilled coffee all over her shoes. That had been a near thing! She

knew that the wretched female flew up and down to
London a lot, but to find herself on the same flight
was hellish. Sarah decided to hang back and make
sure of sitting nowhere near Chloe. Meanwhile, she
would wait in the furthest corner of the lounge.

When the flight was eventually called and the passengers boarded, Sarah's plan worked so well that
she was the last one up the steps. In this she'd been
unwittingly helped by Chloe. Seasoned traveller that
she was, Chloe had taken her time about moving off
and Sarah was unable to collect her raincoat and
hand luggage until the coast was clear. So far, so
good.

Sarah's luck ran out at the other end of the flight
and the two girls collided when collecting their cases
off the carousel. 'What a lovely surprise!' cried
Chloe. 'Of course, you know by now that I thought
you were somebody else that day?'

Somebody else? Was there yet *another* one? Just
how many women had Rory been juggling? 'I know
nothing,' breathed Sarah faintly.

'You mean he didn't explain? Oh, honestly! He's
just too casual by half! I thought you were Moira
somebody.'

'Moira Stirling,' Sarah supplied automatically.

'Yes, that's the one. It was when you said you'd
trained with Rory that I decided you must be the
one he was trying to get off his back. That's why I
gave you the bum's rush the way I did. I was only
trying to help him. You must have thought I was
abominably rude—well, so I was. But I didn't know
about you then. Can you forgive me?'

'Can I...? Yes, why not? It's of no conse-
quence...'

'That's very nice of you. What a pity we didn't meet at Heathrow, though—we could have sat together and had a lovely gossip about my wicked cousin. Have you got transport, Sarah?'

'My car—I left it here...'

'That's all right, then. Otherwise I'm sure Dougal would have— Oh, there he is. And in a hurry as usual. See you!' And she was away, leaving Sarah feeling as though she'd been hit by a whirlwind. So she had, in a way. What was she supposed to make of all that?

'This yours, hen? It's been round twice,' said a friendly official, lifting the last remaining case from the carousel.

'Yes—thank you. I was thinking.'

'No problem,' he returned airily, before sauntering off.

Sarah meandered toward the exit, lost in thought. Chloe's attitude had astounded her. In her place I'd just have nodded, smiled, said hello perhaps, and then walked on by. After all, she couldn't have been too pleased to come in and find a strange woman in residence—Moira or not.

But, then, she's not playing it straight either. That Dougal—who is *he*? He was obviously very pleased to see her...

And she seemed to take it for granted that Rory and I are still friends... Doesn't she know or doesn't she care? And as for wanting to know if I could forgive her. Now, that was really weird...

Sarah bumped into a wire fence and realised that she'd taken the wrong turning for the car park. But even when she'd found her car, she didn't drive away at once. She was too confused, going over and over that extraordinary meeting till she thought her head would burst. When she finally managed to get the key into the ignition, she drove home in a dream.

She woke late next morning. She'd been ages getting to sleep and then she'd had a wonderful dream. Well, more *déjà vu*, really, returning when half in and half out of sleep to that scene in the car park at the foot of Ben Venue after they'd discovered that Rory's car had been stolen.

He'd hugged her tightly and said, 'If there's anybody in the whole world I'd choose to share a tight spot with, it's you.' Surely that meant he saw her as rather special? Later on, the evening had been a bit of an anticlimax, but the next day had been quite wonderful. Most of the next week had been wonderful, too. A lovely warm glow engulfed her at the thought of the Wednesday night.

But then on Sunday Chloe had come.

Supposing I hadn't run away? Supposing I'd stayed and faced it out? Would it have made any difference? But I didn't. And then the next day we quarrelled, so bitterly.

I'm fantasising, she realised painfully. If Rory had really wanted me, he'd have played it all quite differently. When did he ever fail at anything he put his mind to?

Moira and her Stephen were married six weeks after Carrie and Robin. Unlike their wedding, Moira's was a spectacular production at an impossibly posh hotel on the banks of Loch Lomond.

Fiona and Sarah went with Robin and Carrie and, judging by the numbers of cars parked round the

hotel—all the way down the drive and halfway to
Balloch—most of Glasgow had been invited.

'No wonder it's not in a church,' said Robin,
when he saw all the folk milling about in and out
of the building. 'There's not one big enough anywhere in Scotland. Do you suppose they're tying the
knot in the garden?'

'If they are, I'll be watching the proceedings from
a window,' said his true love. 'This hat cost me a
fortune and the forecast is for rain.'

Sarah and Fiona were wearing the outfits they'd
worn for Carrie's wedding. What was good enough
for a friend like Carrie was more than good enough
for Moira. Both girls were surprised to have been
invited at all, never having been among Moira's in-
timates.

'Crowing over us,' Fiona had diagnosed with uncharacteristic waspishness when they'd got their in-
vitations. 'Are we going, Sarah?'

'We most certainly are,' Sarah had answered
firmly. 'Where there's one millionaire, there could
be others—and we're not getting any younger. And
don't you be looking at me like that, Fiona Kerr! I
know we always said we'd only marry for love, but
I for one am older and wiser now!'

'If you say so,' Fiona had answered quietly.

The first familiar face they saw was Rory
Drummond's. He was alone and there was no mistaking his relief when he saw them.

'I thought you were still on holiday, mate,' said
Robin.

'So I am, but I'd not have missed this circus for
a gold clock,' claimed Rory, not quite catching
Sarah's eye. 'It's probably the only chance I'll ever

get to appear in a Hollywood blockbuster—even if it is only as an extra.' Then, with what looked like a supreme effort of will or courtesy, Rory turned to Sarah and asked how she was liking life at the General.

'Very much, thank you,' she answered, copying his careful manner. 'The work is very interesting and the staff most helpful.'

'So you've fallen on your feet, then. And you're certainly looking better of the change,' he added.

'Thank you—you're looking very well yourself. Did I hear Robin say you were on holiday?' Sarah looked round to include Robin and the girls in this difficult, stilted conversation, but somehow they seemed to have got separated.

'You've been on holiday, too,' Rory was saying.

'I— Yes. A visit to my family down in England.'

'I know.' He swallowed visibly. 'My cousin told me she saw you on the plane coming back.'

'At Glasgow airport, actually.'

'Well, whatever.' Again that awkward swallow. Sarah's eyes had homed in on his throat because she couldn't bear to meet his gaze.

'Chloe goes abroad a lot,' he said next, for no apparent reason that Sarah could fathom.

'She must have a very interesting job, then,' she offered desperately.

'It certainly pays well. The thing is, with her being away so much, I've hardly seen her since that weekend you—stayed. At the flat...'

What sort of reply was he expecting to that? 'I suppose that's one of the drawbacks of a high-powered job,' she murmured.

'So I didn't know what passed between you that night until the other day!'

Don't you go putting me in the wrong again, she dared him silently, before telling him robustly, 'She more or less turned me out!'

'I know that—now. You should have told me when—'

'Would it have made any difference?'

'Of course it would! I thought you were just looking for an excuse to…get out. And then, when she said how depressed and forlorn you seemed at the airport, I wondered… I couldn't help wondering if it could—could possibly be anything to do with me. No, of course it wasn't!' he added savagely.

'I suppose it never occurred to you to wonder what my thoughts must have been that night? The sudden appearance of an utterly gorgeous female who seemed to be living with you—acting like she owned the place, telling me to feel free to use the phone—and who seemed to want me out as soon as possible? Of course I bolted! Ever since, though, I've been wishing I'd stayed and faced you down— only I didn't have the bottle!' It was a tremendous relief to get it all said, even though it wouldn't do any good.

'Are you saying that you *minded*? I mean, *really* minded?' His expression was a curious mixture of embarrassment and hope. 'But you were always so confident—so sure of yourself! I waited and waited for some sign of—of involvement, but it never came. So when you walked out like that—and picked that row next day—I accepted the inevitable.

'Then, when I saw Chloe a day or two back and she said she thought— No! She was sure that you were keen on…were upset over me… All rubbish, of course!' he exploded, as the dark clouds which had been massing overhead did the same.

Without realising it, they had wandered away from the crowds and down towards the loch. Rory looked round for cover and drew Sarah into the half-shelter of a boathouse with a verandah before they were completely drenched.

'But it was you,' Sarah said. '*You* were the one who was always so casual. So, of course, I had to act the same way—if that was the way you wanted it.'

'You mean…?' He seized her above the elbows in a bruising grip and she was dazzled by the fierce light in his dark eyes. Her eyelids drooped and with parted lips Sarah waited breathlessly for his kiss.

But Rory hadn't finished talking. 'We're going to get this sorted out once and for all,' he said doggedly. 'It wasn't until you went away with that blasted artist that I got an inkling of how much you meant to me. Gradually, I managed to convince myself that I'd forgotten you, then when I saw you in that car park before the reunion I was…in turmoil. All churned up. But I realised I had to be very, very careful.

'When I heard you'd been seen at the Allanbank—well, it wasn't difficult to arrange a transfer. With no trauma surgery, it's not the most popular posting on the circuit. But having got there, I couldn't decide what line to take with you. So I took my cue from you—all nice and casual. Even after I got you into bed, I didn't feel safe. You still seemed—uncommitted.'

'Well, yes,' she said. 'All those ruddy women buzzing round you! Especially Chloe…'

'I told you—she's my cousin. Nothing more. Anyway, she's besotted with a penniless charmer married to a rich wife he can't afford to leave. Donald somebody…'

'Dougal,' supplied Sarah, remembering the man at the airport. 'Oh, poor Chloe! How terrible for her.'

'Forget Chloe,' he said. 'What about poor Rory and all he's been through?'

Sarah just had to kiss him then—getting more, much more, in return than she'd given. 'Oh, Rory! How could we have been so silly?' she asked breathlessly as soon as she could.

'Because it mattered so much—that's why!' All his hesitation had gone now. 'We were both so scared of doing or saying the wrong thing that we pussy-footed about, getting nowhere! I guess that's what happens when two old friends fall in love.'

'You know all about that, then, do you?' she asked with a saucy tilt of the head and a sparkle in her eyes he'd never thought to see again.

'I do now,' he said firmly, prompting another delicious interlude.

By the time they surfaced the second time, the sun had come out again. 'You know what, Rory?' Sarah whispered against his cheek. 'I think we've probably missed Moira's wedding.'

Rory chuckled wickedly and folded her even closer. 'I can live with that,' he reckoned, 'just so long as we don't miss our own!'

MILLS & BOON®

Makes any time special™

Mills & Boon publish 29 new titles every month. Select from...

Modern Romance™   **Tender Romance**™

Sensual Romance™

Medical Romance™   **Historical Romance**™

The latest triumph from
international bestselling author

Debbie Macomber

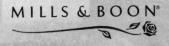

MILLS & BOON®

brings you

PROMISE

*Share the lives—and loves—of the
people in Promise, Texas.
A town with an interesting past
and an exciting future.*

Available from 21st July

4 FREE
books and a surprise gift!

We would like to take this opportunity to thank you for reading this Mills & Boon® book by offering you the chance to take FOUR more specially selected titles from the Medical Romance™ series absolutely FREE! We're also making this offer to introduce you to the benefits of the Reader Service™—

★ FREE home delivery
★ FREE gifts and competitions
★ FREE monthly Newsletter
★ Exclusive Reader Service discounts
★ Books available before they're in the shops

Accepting these FREE books and gift places you under no obligation to buy, you may cancel at any time, even after receiving your free shipment. Simply complete your details below and return the entire page to the address below. *You don't even need a stamp!*

YES! Please send me 4 free Medical Romance books and a surprise gift. I understand that unless you hear from me, I will receive 6 superb new titles every month for just £2.40 each, postage and packing free. I am under no obligation to purchase any books and may cancel my subscription at any time. The free books and gift will be mine to keep in any case.

M0ZEA

Ms/Mrs/Miss/Mr ....Initials.....................................
                                                     BLOCK CAPITALS PLEASE

Surname ....

Address ....

....

....Postcode................................

Send this whole page to:
UK: FREEPOST CN81, Croydon, CR9 3WZ
EIRE: PO Box 4546, Kilcock, County Kildare (stamp required)